The AMISH *Millionaire*

PART 1 OF 6

WANDA & BRUNSTETTER

& JEAN BRUNSTETTER

The

ENGLISH
SON

SHILOH RUN PRESS

An Imprint of Barbour Publishing, Inc.

Print ISBN 978-1-63409-203-6

eBook Editions:
Adobe Digital Edition (.epub) 978-1-63409-760-4
Kindle and MobiPocket Edition (.prc) 978-1-63409-761-1

Cover design: Müllerhaus Publishing Arts Inc., www.mullerhaus.net
Cover photography: Richard Brunstetter III, RB III Studios

Published by Shiloh Run Press, an imprint of Barbour Publishing, Inc.,
P.O. Box 719, Uhrichsville, Ohio 44683, www.shilohrunpress.com

*Our mission is to publish and distribute inspirational products offering
exceptional value and biblical encouragement to the masses.*

 Member of the
Evangelical Christian
Publishers Association

Printed in the United States of America.

Byler Family Tree

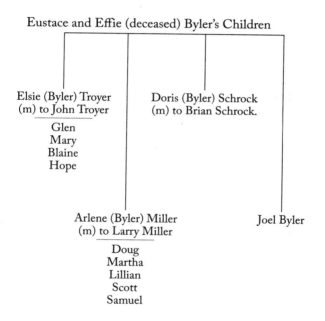

Eustace and Effie (deceased) Byler's Children

Elsie (Byler) Troyer
(m) to John Troyer

Glen
Mary
Blaine
Hope

Doris (Byler) Schrock
(m) to Brian Schrock.

Arlene (Byler) Miller
(m) to Larry Miller

Doug
Martha
Lillian
Scott
Samuel

Joel Byler

CHAPTER 1

Akron, Ohio

One thing Joel Byler couldn't stand was a dirty car. While the vehicle he'd bought today might be a classic, the exterior needed some help.

Joel was thankful his girlfriend, Kristi Palmer, had gone shopping in Holmes County with her mother and wouldn't be back until Sunday evening. That would give him all weekend to spend with his new car. As soon as he got it washed, he might see if Tom Hunter was free to take a test drive with him.

Joel leaned against his work truck and stared at the tuxedo-black 1967 Corvette Stingray convertible. What a beaut! Even with a layer of dust, it was any man's dream. Well, Joel's anyway. He'd wanted a car like this for a long time and had been watching the ads, as well as going to classic car auctions every chance he got. The sale he'd attended this morning had been surprisingly successful. When this gem came up for auction, Joel couldn't resist. A few others apparently wanted the Corvette as badly as he did, because the bidding shot up quickly.

Before Joel realized it, the highest bid was $200,000. In desperation, he upped the bid by $50,000 and won. The only downside was he'd gone way over his budget to get the car, even though with its 435-horsepower engine, the model in this good condition usually sold for more than $300,000.

As a general contractor, cash availability was often feast or famine. Before the most recent job—a big office complex—Joel's cash flow had been on the meager side. Now, after using more than half the money he'd earned from that job to buy the car, the amount left over was not enough to pay all his subcontractors. But Joel felt certain his bid on a huge upcoming job would be chosen and the advance from that would get him out of the jam he'd put himself in. Once he got paid, he'd have money to spare, even after he paid everyone else. And he would finally be able to get the engagement ring Kristi deserved. Joel had already proposed, and she'd said yes, but he didn't have the funds for a ring yet— at least not one big enough to prove his love for her. Kristi had assured Joel she didn't need a fancy ring, but Joel wanted her to have the best. They'd both been saving money for their future together and would eventually use it on a down payment for a house.

Joel turned his attention to the Corvette again. The first order of business was to wash the outside. He paused a minute to study himself in the side mirror, realizing he, too, needed some sprucing up. Besides the streaks of dirt on his face, his thick, dark hair could use a trim. He'd have to get it done before seeing Kristi—and even-up his short beard. As a business owner, he needed to make a good impression on his customers, but he didn't care about his appearance when he was at home.

Joel turned on the outdoor faucet, but before he could grab the end of the hose, it started twirling around under the water pressure, and a blast of chilly water hit Joel square in the face. It also gave his clothes a good soaking, especially the T-shirt, now sticking to him like glue.

He jumped back and wiped his eyes, then grabbed the flailing hose and pointed it at the Corvette. This was not the way he'd planned to take a bath, even though the cool water felt good.

It took Joel almost an hour to get the car clean and dry. He used a sponge to clean off a smudge he'd missed and then rubbed the spot shiny clean with a chamois. About to go inside his single-wide mobile home, Joel paused, watching his friend Tom pull up. *Perfect timing.* Joel grinned.

Tom got out of his SUV and sauntered up the driveway, where Joel's new car was parked. "Wow! Where'd ya get the good-looking Vette?" Tom let out a low whistle while checking it out.

"Got it at a car auction this morning." Joel pointed to the shiny black hood. "What do you think?"

Tom blew out his breath. "You've either come into a large sum of money, or you're deep in debt. She's sweet all right. Bet this classic had to be expensive."

"It was," Joel admitted.

"So how'd ya swing it?"

"I recently got paid for a big job I completed, so I had the money to pay cash." He chuckled, pulling his fingers through his scruffy short beard. "Well, to be honest, I actually wrote a check."

Tom continued to eyeball the car, walking all around it and then opening the passenger door. "Why don't ya take me for a spin? I bet this Vette has got some get-up-and-go."

"You read my mind. I was planning to drive over to your place to show it to you." Joel tugged on his wet shirttail, wringing out the moisture still left. "Give me a few minutes to get cleaned up, and then we'll take a ride."

"Sounds good." Tom followed Joel up to his single-wide. "Mind telling me what you paid for the car?"

Joel hesitated a few seconds. "Umm. . .got it for $250,000."

Tom's mouth dropped open, and he blinked his pale blue eyes a couple of times. "You're kidding, right?"

"Nope. It was my final bid."

"Wow, at this rate you'll be living in a mobile home the rest of your life and never get your dream house built, let alone marry your girlfriend. When Kristi sees your new purchase, I wonder what she'll have to say."

Joel cringed. "I don't plan on letting her see it. At least not right away. So please don't say anything, okay?"

Tom slid his fingers across his lips. "She won't hear it from me. That's a promise." Pointing to the Corvette, Tom's eyes darkened. "How you gonna keep something like this baby hidden from her, Joel? Doesn't Kristi ever go in your garage?"

"I'm not keeping it there. I'm gonna put the Vette in my shop, under a tarp." Joel's deceit didn't bother him that much. He figured he'd tell Kristi about the car when the time was right—maybe after he'd given her a ring and a wedding date had been set. They could go out to dinner in the Corvette to celebrate.

Berlin, Ohio

"Sure wish I had enough money saved up to buy an Amish quilt," Kristi commented as she and her mother entered a quilt shop on Main Street. "All the extra money I make goes into the joint account Joel and I opened eight months ago. I won't touch that—not without Joel's permission. We made an agreement when we first opened the account not to take out a penny of the money unless an emergency arose, and then, only with the other person's approval."

Mom tipped her head. "What is this savings account for?"

"Our future—together."

"Has he asked you to marry him?"

Kristi nodded.

Mom took hold of Kristi's left hand. "I don't see a diamond sparkling back at me."

"He hasn't bought me an engagement ring yet, but I'm sure I'll be wearing one soon."

Deep wrinkles formed across Mom's forehead. Her blue eyes, mirroring Kristi's, had lost their sparkle. "I'm sure you're aware of what the Bible says about being unequally yoked with unbelievers."

"Yes, Mom, I'm aware of what the Bible says, plus you have mentioned it often enough."

"But you're not listening. If you were, you would have broken up with Joel by now."

"I love him, Mom. Besides, he's gone to church with me every Sunday for the past two months."

"Going to church and becoming a believer are two different things. Has Joel told you he's become a Christian?"

Kristi shook her head. "Not in so many words, but—"

"He might only be going to church for your sake—to make you believe he's something he's not. Joel seems to be nice enough, but from what I can tell, he's not spiritually grounded."

Irritation welled in Kristi's soul. She wished her mother would stop harping on this. Mom didn't realize how much Kristi loved Joel. She apparently didn't see the good in him, either. "I doubt Joel's only going to church for my sake, Mom. He promised he'd go to church tomorrow, even though I won't be with him because you and I will be worshipping at the Mennonite church we saw near our hotel in Walnut Creek."

Mom didn't say anything as she moved to the next aisle full of more quilts, but Kristi was fully aware of her mother's reservations about Joel. Kristi pursed her lips. *Aren't we supposed to look for the good in others? How come Mom can't do that with Joel?*

She rummaged through her purse to find her cell phone. When she touched the smooth object with her fingers, Kristi clenched the phone and took it out of her bag. *Maybe I ought to call Joel and remind him about going to church. No!* She immediately dropped the phone back in. *He might think I was treating him like a child. He told me he would go, and I believe him.*

Kristi had learned many things about Joel in the year and a half they'd been dating. One thing stood out more than the rest: He didn't like to be told what to do. When she'd first met him, he wasn't willing to attend church at all. At least he went with her now, and that's what mattered. While Joel didn't talk about spiritual things, Kristi had noticed how easily he could find scripture passages when the pastor preached his messages. When she'd asked Joel about this, he'd merely explained he'd grown up going to church and the Bible had been crammed down his throat. When she'd asked for more details, he'd said he didn't want to talk about it.

Joel never spoke of his family. Kristi couldn't help wondering why. Since he had asked her to marry him, she figured it was time to meet his folks. When she'd brought up the topic, Joel informed her that his family was different, and Kristi wouldn't have anything in common with them; then he'd quickly changed the subject. Kristi realized it was best not to press the issue and hadn't brought it up again. But it didn't keep her from wondering what Joel's family was like and how they would be different from her. Someday, when Joel was in the right mood, she would broach the subject again. It wouldn't be right to marry Joel when she had no knowledge of his family other than being told they were different. Surely, Joel would want to invite them to the wedding.

Shaking her thoughts aside, Kristi moved to the next aisle, where Mom stood, studying a quilted wall hanging. Her mother had recently gotten her auburn hair cut in a shorter style. It made her look younger than her fifty years. "Goodness, gracious, even this quilted piece is expensive," Mom commented when Kristi joined her.

"The price is a shocker, but it's worth every penny." Kristi pointed to the nearly invisible hand stitching. "A lot of work goes into making one of these."

"I can see that." Mom shook her head, clicking her tongue. "I can sew a straight seam, but I might not have the patience to make a quilt, or even a hanging such as this."

"If I wasn't working long hours at the nursing home, I'd try making a quilt." Kristi smiled. "Of course, someone would have to teach me, because even with a quilt pattern, I would have no idea where to begin."

"It's apparent how important nursing is to you. Honestly, though, Kristi, you need to make time to do some fun things for yourself."

"I do," Kristi was quick to respond. "In fact, Joel and I are going out for supper one evening next week."

Mom's lips compressed. "I wasn't talking about going on dates. I meant doing something creative just for you. They give quilting lessons here in the store. Maybe the two of us could sign up for one."

Kristi mulled over her mother's suggestion. "It's a nice idea, but I'd have to attend on a Saturday, and I like to keep my weekends free to spend with Joel."

"You're here now, and he didn't object." Her brows furrowed. "Or did he?"

Kristi shook her head. "A quilt class would probably mean coming here several Saturdays in a row in order to complete the quilt. Besides, it's a bit of a drive from Akron down here to Holmes County, and as I said, Joel and I usually do something together on Saturdays."

Mom held up her hand. "I understand. You want a quilt, but you can't afford to buy one, and you don't want to be away from Joel long enough to make one."

Kristi cringed. The curt tone of her mother's voice was all she needed as a reminder of how much Mom disapproved of Joel. *She and Dad don't know Joel as well as I do. He's smart, good-looking, and a successful businessman. Once he's fully committed to the Lord, he will make a great husband.*

"Why don't we get some lunch?" Kristi suggested, realizing she needed to change the subject. "There's a restaurant next to our hotel in Walnut Creek we should try."

"Since you mentioned it, I am kind of hungry." Mom moved up the aisle, and Kristi followed. After lunch she hoped to check out a few of the Amish-owned businesses in the area.

Kristi wasn't sure why, but she was fascinated with the Amish culture and wanted to learn as much as possible about it.

Walnut Creek, Ohio

"How's your meal?" Mom asked as she and Kristi sat at a table near a window in Der Dutchman Restaurant.

Kristi licked her lips. "The chicken is delicious—crispy on the outside and tender inside. I'm glad we chose this place to have lunch."

"Yes, and our waitress has been so attentive." Mom motioned to the young Amish woman who had left their table after filling the glasses with fresh iced tea. "I'll make sure to leave her a nice tip."

Kristi smiled. Mom had always been good about leaving generous tips when she'd had exceptional service. It was a good example for Kristi, and she remembered to do the same.

As they continued eating their meal, Mom mentioned the beautiful weather. "We picked the perfect time for this weekend getaway— nice even temperature and not much humidity, which is unusual for August."

"I agree." Kristi blotted her lips with a napkin. "Some summers it's been so hot and humid it was hard to be outdoors." She glanced out the window at a passing horse and buggy, wondering how it would feel to ride in one of them. She'd seen an Amish man across the street from the hotel offering rides for a reasonable price. Maybe after lunch, before they got back in Kristi's car, she would suggest they take a buggy ride.

Before taking a sip of iced tea, Kristi looked out another window, where the horse and buggies were parked. She watched in awe as an elderly couple was about to leave. The Amish woman held the reins of the horse while her husband, a bit shaky on his feet, got in. Once he was settled in the buggy, she handed him the reins. Keeping her eyes peeled to the window, Kristi watched as he backed the horse up and guided their buggy toward the road.

"Is there anything else I can bring for you?" their waitress asked, stepping up to the table. "A piece of pie or some ice cream?"

"Both sound good, Doris, but I'm too full." Mom nudged Kristi's arm. "How about you? Do you have room for dessert?"

Kristi placed both hands on her stomach, glancing one last time out the window. "As good at it sounds, I don't have space for another bite."

When the waitress smiled, Kristi noticed her flawless complexion, offset by dark brown eyes with long lashes. Not much of her hair showed under her stiff white head covering, but what did show was a dark brown color.

I wonder how it would feel to dress in plain clothes. Kristi looked down at her pale green blouse and darker green capris. She was tempted to ask the young woman if she wore the white cap all the time or only when she was in public. Mom would have been embarrassed by her blunt question, and the Amish woman might think she was rude.

"Thank you for coming in. You can pay your bill up front." The young woman placed the piece of paper on the table beside Mom's plate. Apparently she assumed Mom would be the one paying the bill.

After the waitress walked away, Kristi leaned closer to Mom and whispered, "How come you called her Doris? I don't believe she ever told us her name."

"She was wearing a name tag—Doris Schrock. Didn't you see it?"

"I guess not. I did notice her pretty brown eyes, though. They're almost the same color as Joel's."

Mom quirked an eyebrow. "You're comparing the Amish woman to Joel? Is he all you have on your mind today, Kristi?"

"Of course not. I thought of Joel when I saw her pretty brown eyes."

"Maybe they're related. He does have an Amish-sounding last name."

"But you said her last name was Schrock, not Byler."

Mom heaved a sigh. "I was only teasing, Kristi. Joel is obviously not Amish. He drives a car, uses electricity in his mobile home, and dresses like other non-Amish men do."

Kristi crossed her arms. "I know Joel pretty well, Mom, and besides, this is a silly discussion." She reached for the check. "Lunch is on me, and when we leave here, I want to go on a buggy ride."

Mom's forehead wrinkled. "I thought we were going to do some more shopping. Didn't you say you wanted to check out a few of the Amish-owned businesses in the area?"

"Yes, I do, but we can do it after the buggy ride."

"You go ahead if you want to. I'm not interested in going for a ride. I'll sit on the bench in front of the hotel and wait for you."

"Never mind. If you're not going to do it, then neither am I." Kristi pushed away from the table. "Let's head for Charm. I hear there's a cheese shop there. I may pick some up to take home."

"Good idea. I'll buy some cheese, too. Your dad would be happy if I came home with a brick of Colby."

As Kristi made her way to the front of the restaurant, a vision of Joel flashed across her mind. *I wonder if he'd like to make a trip to Holmes County with me sometime. When I see him next week, I'll ask.*

CHAPTER 2

Akron

Stretching his arms behind his back to massage the knots, Joel ambled into the kitchen. He'd spent all weekend joy-riding in his new Corvette and had gone to bed late last night. Joel had been with Tom most of Saturday. On Sunday, he'd gone to Cleveland to see an old friend. When he returned home, he was tired and hadn't taken the time to check his voice mail. He'd had his cell phone with him all weekend, of course, but didn't want to be disturbed with any work-related calls, so he'd kept it muted.

Joel picked up his phone from the kitchen counter, where he'd plugged it in to charge before going to bed. *Guess I'd better see if I have any messages. Kristi may have called.*

Scrolling through his phone with his index finger, Joel saw that Kristi had called. He typed in the password and pressed the phone against his ear to hear the message she'd left on his voicemail. Apparently, she had tried calling him when she got home last evening and couldn't wait to tell him about the fun she'd had in Amish country.

Joel grimaced. The last time he'd paid a visit to Holmes County, he'd come away appreciating his truck and mid-sized car. Now Joel had another vehicle to brag about. He hoped the Corvette would be the first of many classic cars he'd own. Of course, he'd have to make a lot more money for his dream to become reality.

Joel had prepared for getting more cars by building a spacious five-car garage. The added space at the back of his shop would also be utilized when his collection grew. Since Joel owned two acres of land, he had the option of building another garage or additional shop, if and when it became necessary. His dream was to keep some cars for show and to ride around in, but some he would fix up and sell for a tidy profit. He planned to keep the Corvette, however, since he had dreamed for a long time of owning one.

Joel's passion for cars began when he was a teenager. After he'd gotten his first job and saved enough money, he'd bought a classy-looking red convertible. His family hadn't approved, but it had turned many other heads. Eventually, he'd been forced to sell it. That was another story, but Joel didn't want to dwell on the details. He had better things to do today, starting with checking the rest of his messages.

He found a few work-related calls—some from subcontractors with questions about a small job he was supposed to do later this week. Another was from Carl and Mary Blankenship, an elderly couple who wanted Joel to give them a bid on a partial bathroom remodel. The things the Blankenships wanted done wouldn't take long, nor bring in much money, so Joel would handle the job himself. He hoped to hear something soon about the bigger job he'd bid on. Once he got the go-ahead, he'd get his subcontractors started on it right away.

One thing was for sure; he wouldn't tell Kristi about the car. She might think he was never going to buy her a ring and would probably say he'd been foolish for spending so much money on a car he would drive occasionally. Good thing she never had any reason to snoop around in his shop, and he'd make sure she never did. At least not until they were married.

Joel glanced at the clock above his refrigerator. Kristi had probably left for work already, so he would wait and call her back sometime this evening. Right now, he needed to eat breakfast and head out the door.

As Joel drove his pickup toward the Blankenships', he decided to take a side road. It wouldn't hurt to check out the jobsite he figured he would be starting soon. His bid had been reasonable, and Joel felt sure he'd been chosen to do the job. He saw right away that the land had been fenced, in readiness for the project to begin. If by some chance the owner was there, Joel could ask when he wanted him to begin the building process. Once everything had been finalized, he would request half the money now and the rest when the job was complete. Even the first half would be a nice chunk, allowing Joel to pay all his subcontractors what he owed from the last job he'd done, with some left over for expenses and Kristi's ring.

When Joel approached the jobsite, already cleared and excavated, he drew in a sharp breath, unable to believe his eyes. Tacked to the fence closest to the road was another general contractor's construction sign.

"This better not mean what it looks like," Joel muttered. He pulled over and grabbed his cell phone, hurriedly making the call. "Hey, Andy, it's Joel Byler. I'm sitting in front of the property you bought for your new business and am wondering why another contractor's sign is tacked to the fence."

"Didn't my secretary call you, Joel?"

"No, she did not. What was she supposed to tell me?"

"I gave the job to Martin's Construction. He came in with a lower bid and is able to start working on the project right away."

Joel clenched his teeth so hard he felt it all the way to his head. "But you promised me the job, and I'm able to start on it now, too."

"I made no promises, Joel. Only said it sounded like a fair bid and I'd get back to you."

Joel's hand shook as he switched his cell phone to the other ear. He couldn't lose this job; he had too much at stake. "Listen, Andy, why don't you let me refigure things a bit; I'm sure I can knock some off my original figures."

"Sorry, but I've already accepted Jim Martin's bid. The contract is signed, and he'll be starting the job tomorrow morning."

"Are you sure? I mean—"

"I have to go now, Joel. Another call's coming in." The phone clicked off before Joel could say another word.

Pounding his fist on the truck's dash, Joel shouted, "What am I gonna do now? All I have scheduled are a few small jobs. Those won't earn enough money to pay even half what I owe. How am I going to get any of my subs to work for me if I can't pay 'em what they've got coming?"

Joel would have to figure out a solution to this problem soon, or he'd really be in a pickle. The only sensible thing would be to sell the new car, but it might take a while to find someone willing to pay what it was worth. Besides, Joel didn't want to part with the Vette. No, there had to be some other way.

Kristi smiled as she put her grocery items away, reliving the past weekend with her mother. Shopping was something she and Mom had always enjoyed doing together. Even when Kristi was a child, she'd liked to shop. Every time Mom put on her coat, Kristi would ask, "Are we going shopping, Mom?"

Chuckling, Kristi checked her phone messages. She'd been running late this morning and, in her haste, had left her cell phone on the kitchen table.

Yesterday evening, when she'd returned from Holmes County, Kristi had called Joel and left a message, so she was eager to see if he had responded.

Disappointment flooded over her when she saw no message. Hadn't he checked his voice mail since last night? If he had, surely he would have returned her call. This wasn't like Joel at all.

Kristi punched in Joel's number, feeling relief when he answered.

"Hey, Joel, it's me. Did you get my message from last night?"

"Uh...yeah, I did. Sorry for not responding. I've...uh...been kinda busy."

"That's okay. I was wondering if you were free to have supper with me tonight. On my way home, I picked up a couple of steaks and some baking potatoes; so, instead of going out, I thought we could eat here."

"Not tonight, Kristi. I've got a bunch of paperwork I need to get done."

"Paperwork? I thought you were going to work on it over the weekend." She couldn't hide her disappointment. Joel had previously said they would get together one night this week, and she was anxious to tell him about her trip to Holmes County.

"I. . .umm. . . had a lot to go over, but unfortunately, I didn't get it all done."

"How about tomorrow night? The steaks will keep till then."

Silence on the other end.

"Joel, are you still there? Did you hear what I said?"

"Yeah, I'm thinking is all."

Kristi reached up and released her hair from the ponytail she'd worn to work today. "Are you thinking about whether you want to come for supper?" She couldn't imagine he wouldn't. Joel always seemed to enjoy her home-cooked meals.

"No. . .uh. . . I have a few other things on my mind right now."

"Want to talk about it?" Kristi felt concern. It wasn't like Joel to be so distant or evasive. She wondered if he was irritated because she'd spent the weekend with her mother instead of him. She was about to ask when he spoke again.

"There's nothing to talk about, Kristi. I had a rough day, but I'll be okay." Joel cleared his throat. "Tomorrow evening for supper is fine with me. What time do you want me to come over?"

"Is five thirty too early, or would you rather make it six?"

"Let's shoot for six. Is there anything I can bring?"

"A hearty appetite. I bought some whoopie pies at the bakery outside of Berlin, so we'll have those for dessert."

"Okay. See you then." Joel hung up before Kristi had the chance to say goodbye. Something was definitely wrong, but if Joel didn't want to talk about it, there wasn't much she could do. Kristi felt hurt because Joel hadn't even said he loved her, which he usually did before they hung up. Could the thrill of their romance be fading? *Maybe I'm overly sensitive today.*

"I hope Joel's willing to talk about this when he comes here tomorrow night," Kristi murmured. She didn't want to make any assumptions that may not even be true.

Feeling uptight, Kristi decided to go for a run. Physical activity usually helped whenever she was stressed. She quickly changed into her jogging clothes, put her hair back in a ponytail, and headed out the door.

Kristi had only run a few blocks when she saw her friend Sandy Clemons running in the opposite direction. Sandy was into fitness even more than Kristi, and they sometimes ran together. When the young woman drew closer, they both stopped running and stood on the corner to talk.

"How's it going?" Sandy asked, pushing a strand of her chin-length, naturally blond hair behind her ear. "I missed seeing you in church yesterday."

"I went shopping in Holmes County with my mom on Saturday. After spending the night in Walnut Creek, we attended a Mennonite church near our hotel."

"Sounds like a fun outing."

Kristi nodded. "We had such a good time. I'm anxious to go there again—maybe next time with Joel."

"Where was Joel yesterday? I didn't see him at church."

Kristi bent her knee back to rub the calf of her leg, where a muscle had begun to spasm. The cramp was her fault. The weather had turned a lot warmer from the past weekend, and she was sorry she'd left her condo in a rush, forgetting her water bottle. "Are you sure Joel wasn't there, Sandy? When I told him I was going away for the weekend, he said he wouldn't skip church."

"If he was there, I didn't see him. But even though I'm up front leading the worship team, I don't always notice everyone in the congregation. When I get into a worshipful mood, I focus on God, not on the crowd."

"That's where it should be, alright." Kristi didn't voice her concerns, but she had a feeling Joel hadn't gone to church. When they'd talked on the phone, he'd said he had done paperwork, so there was a good chance he'd spent Saturday and Sunday working on it. Of course, it was no excuse. Kristi had been brought up to believe in the importance of going to church. Unless she was sick or something unexpected came up, she made an effort to be there.

"Guess I'd better finish my jogging session so I can go home and start supper before my hubby gets home from work." Sandy gave Kristi a hug and started running again.

As Kristi continued her run, she made a decision. Tomorrow night when Joel came for supper, she would ask if he'd gone to church. Surely he would tell her the truth.

CHAPTER 3

Kristi glanced at the clock and frowned. It was six thirty. Joel was supposed to be here thirty minutes ago. The yummy smell of baked potatoes coming from the oven made her stomach growl. She was eager to eat. The potatoes would stay warm in the oven. Fortunately, she hadn't put the steaks on the grill yet, thinking it would be best to wait until Joel arrived.

Kristi left the kitchen and peeked out the living-room window. No sign of Joel's car or work truck in her condo driveway. She looked at her wristwatch and groaned. *I hope he didn't forget. Wonder if I should call him.*

She reached for her cell phone and was about to make the call when Joel pulled in. She hurried to the deck at the back of her condo and turned on the gas grill, which would give it time to warm up before Joel came in.

"Sorry I'm late," Joel apologized when she let him inside. "I had to make a few phone calls after work and time got away from me." He leaned down and gave her a kiss.

"It's okay." She smiled up at him, reminded once again what an attractive man he was. His thick, dark hair with eyebrows to match and

33

those expressive chocolate-brown eyes were enough to turn any woman's head. Of course, his good looks weren't the only reason Kristi had fallen in love with Joel. He was intelligent, a hard worker, had a good business head, and his attentiveness made her feel good about herself. Joel also enjoyed jogging, which was one of Kristi's passions. She'd always believed in being physically fit—ate healthy foods and exercised regularly. The day she'd first met Joel at a fitness center in Akron, Kristi wanted to get to know him better. After a few more visits, Joel had asked her out.

"Umm. . .guess I'd better put the steaks on the grill." Pushing her dreamy thoughts aside, Kristi headed for the kitchen, and Joel followed.

"If there's something else you need to do, I can put the steaks on for you," he offered.

Kristi smiled. "You can if you want to, but the salad is in the refrigerator, the potatoes are in the oven, and the table's set, so I don't have anything else to do. Why don't we both go on the deck and watch the steaks? It'll give us a chance to visit while they're cooking. In fact, I'll get some iced tea to drink while we're sitting outside."

"Sounds good to me." Joel took the steaks out to the deck, and when Kristi showed up with their drinks a few minutes later, the meat was sizzling on the grill. She placed their glasses on the small table then took a seat in one of the wicker chairs she'd recently purchased.

Shielding her eyes from the setting sun, Kristi smiled at Joel. "I'm anxious to tell you about my weekend and hear about yours."

Holding his glass against his flushed face, Joel sat in the chair beside her. "There's not much to tell about my weekend. It was basically pretty boring."

"What about church? Did you go there Sunday morning?" Kristi already suspected the answer, but wanted to give him a chance to explain.

Joel shook his head.

"How come?" Feeling the heat and humidity of the summer evening, Kristie fanned her face with her hand.

"I had planned to go, but I had too much paperwork."

"I realize your work is important, but couldn't you have taken an hour out to attend church? You promised you would go, remember?" Despite her irritation, Kristi appreciated the fact that Joel hadn't lied about not going. If there was one thing she wouldn't tolerate, it was someone lying to her.

Frowning, his tone quickly sharpened. "Don't start nagging me, Kristi. I get enough of it from my customers." He stood abruptly and went over to the grill to check the meat.

She flinched. Joel had never talked to her so harshly before. It took her by surprise.

After he added some seasoning to the steaks, Joel stood quietly, looking out behind her place. Kristi wondered what thoughts were rolling around in his head. Even after he took a seat beside her again, he said nothing.

"I–I'm sorry, Joel." She placed her hand gently on his arm. "I didn't mean to sound bossy."

"No problem."

Kristi got up to flip the steaks, and as the flames shot upward, a piece of hot gristle popped out. "Ouch!" She jumped back when a tiny piece landed on her arm.

"Are you okay?" Joel bolted out of his chair.

"I'm alright—just startled is all." Kristi felt reassured, seeing the depth of worry in his expression and knowing he really cared. This was the Joel she'd come to know and love.

"I'll be right back." Joel rushed inside and returned with an ice cube wrapped in a napkin. "Here, sit down and put this on the red mark. I'll tend to the steaks." His face softened. "I'm sorry I barked at you before. Guess I'm kinda testy tonight."

"Bad day at work?"

He gave a nod. "Thought I'd landed a pretty big job, but another contractor came in with a lower bid."

"I suppose it happens sometimes. Do you have other jobs lined up?"

"A few, but nothing big." The worry lines on his forehead returned, causing Kristi concern.

"Let's pray about this, should we?" she asked.

"You mean right now?"

"Yes. There's no time like the present." Kristi reached for Joel's hand and bowed her head. "Heavenly Father, Joel is disappointed because he didn't get that job, but we're trusting You to bring an even bigger job along for him. Thank You for hearing our prayer and for all You do on our behalf. Amen."

Kristi opened her eyes and smiled at Joel. He smiled back, but it appeared to be forced. Didn't he realize no matter how big the problem seemed, God could take care of it and provide for his needs? She hated to admit it, but this was an indication of Joel not having a strong faith in God. Perhaps it would come in time.

Berlin

Doris Schrock stepped from her kitchen to the back porch, hoping to find some cool air. Not a single leaf in the yard moved. As far as she could see, everything was still. The stifling heat and humidity felt like thick fog. The restaurant where she worked in Walnut Creek had air-conditioning, so she'd been comfortable all day. But after putting a roast in her oven for supper here at home, the already warm kitchen had become almost unbearable. If the weather was cooler, she and her husband, Brian, could eat outside. But unless a sudden breeze came up, it would be as bad as eating in the house.

She sighed deeply and stepped back inside. Brian should be in from his chores soon, and then they could eat.

While Doris waited, she filled their glasses with iced tea and placed them on the table beside their plates—plates that used to belong to her mother.

Unexpectedly, she thought of her brother, wondering what he was doing for dinner this evening. *I wonder if he would come if I invited him here for a meal. It's been awhile since any of the family has seen him. Does he miss us at all?*

Using a potholder, she opened the oven door to check on the roast. A wave of hot air hit her in the face. She waved the worst of it away, then poked the potatoes and carrots with a fork. They were done, and so was the meat. The supper she'd planned was probably not the best choice on an uncomfortable evening like this. Using the oven made the kitchen even more stifling. BLT's would have been easier, but since the meat had already thawed, Doris didn't have much choice. There wasn't anything to do now except wait for Brian.

She took a seat at the table to read the latest edition of *The Bargain Hunter*. It seemed like there were more ads than usual from people wanting to sell baby items. Several advertisements were for cribs, strollers, and high chairs.

Tears pooled in her eyes. Short of a miracle, she would never own any of those things. Doris and Brian had been married six years, but God had not blessed them with children. It didn't seem fair that Arlene, who was thirty-two, recently had a baby. Arlene's pregnancy had been a surprise, since her youngest child, Scott, was eight years old.

"But God knows best," she murmured. "At least that's what Mama used to say."

Doris's tears dripped onto her cheeks. Her

mother had died two years ago, but she still missed her so much. Dad missed her, too. The last time Doris went to his house, she'd caught him sitting on the sofa in the living room, looking at Mama's rocking chair while talking to her as if she was still there.

She and her sisters had tried talking their father into selling his house and moving in with one of them. But Dad insisted on staying in the home he and Mama had lived in since they first got married. Doris couldn't really blame him. If something were to happen to Brian, she wouldn't want to leave this house, either, even though it was small and needed a lot of repairs. They'd planned to add on, but with Brian so busy working for a local carpenter and completing all his chores at home, he hadn't had time to build an addition. Still, this little house held memories, making her understand how Dad felt.

I suppose it doesn't matter. Since we have no children, we don't really need a bigger place. Doris reached for a napkin and wiped her damp cheeks. *I will not give in to self-pity. At least Brian and I both have jobs. A lot of people in our community are struggling financially, so I'm grateful.*

Hearing her husband's footsteps on the stairs outside, Doris got up from the table and collected herself. She would not let Brian see her tears. She'd done too much crying already.

Akron

As the evening wore on, Joel became antsy. He wanted to be with Kristi and have a nice evening, but right now, he couldn't deal with her questions. Before their meal, she'd questioned him about going to church. During the meal, she'd asked not once, but several times, if everything was alright between them, saying he seemed kind of sullen this evening. As they sat eating their dessert, Joel had assured her everything was fine, but not more than five minutes had passed, and she'd begun firing questions again.

"I told you before, nothing is wrong. Now can we talk about something else?" he snapped, a bit too harshly. Truth was, Joel was worried about his financial situation, and talking about it only made him feel worse. What he wanted to do was go home, hop in the Corvette, and leave his troubles behind on the open road.

"You haven't asked about my weekend." Kristi looked at him with misty eyes. "Don't you want to hear about the shopping trip I took with my mom to Holmes County?"

Not wanting to hurt her feelings, Joel nodded. He was drawn in by her eyes, which suddenly looked three shades bluer. "Sure, honey. Tell me what you bought." He fingered her beautiful auburn hair.

"Actually, I didn't buy much. What I really wanted was an Amish-made quilt, but the ones Mom and I looked at were too expensive." She paused to take a bite of her whoopie pie. "But I did buy a few quilted potholders. Those will look nice in our kitchen someday."

Our kitchen. Joel groaned inwardly, taking a toothpick from his shirt pocket. With his current financial situation, it could be some time before he had enough money to buy Kristi an engagement ring, let alone set a wedding date. *If Mom were still alive, she'd say I was foolhardy for buying the Corvette. Maybe I was, but I couldn't pass up the opportunity to own something I'd been wanting for a long time. Besides, how was I to know my bid on that job wasn't the lowest? Thought it was a sure thing.* Joel clenched his teeth until his jaw ached. *Guess it's what I get for not looking before I leaped. I need to figure a way out of this jam. Once I get some good money coming in, I'll be fine again.*

CHAPTER 4

Millersburg, Ohio

I can't believe how much produce my garden has yielded this summer," Elsie Troyer commented as she stood at her kitchen sink, washing beets.

Elsie's sister, Arlene Miller, had been helping her can some of the bounty all morning. Tomorrow they would go to Arlene's home in Farmerstown and do the same with her crop.

The skin around Arlene's blue eyes crinkled. "I am ever so thankful my older girls are willing to watch the *boppli*, or I'd never get anything done at home, much less be able to help you. Of course, once Martha and Lillian start back to school, I'll be on my own with the baby and most household chores."

"If Mary didn't have a job cleaning house, I'm sure she'd be willing to watch little Samuel, and so would Hope." Elsie glanced out the kitchen window, where eleven-year-old Hope was busy pulling weeds in the garden. "If Hope came into the kitchen with the smell of pickled beets cooking, she'd plug her nose and say, 'Eww. . .those are *ekelhaft*!'"

"Oh, that's right; your youngest daughter has never liked beets. It's no wonder she thinks the odor is disgusting."

"I'd thought about bringing Samuel with me today, but Martha and Lillian needed to clean their rooms, so they'll take turns minding the baby."

Elsie washed another beet and placed it in the bowl for Arlene to cut. "Yesterday I went over to Dad's to clean his house."

"How's he doing?"

"He left a few minutes after I got there. Said he had an auction to go to." Elsie wrinkled her nose. "I can't believe how much junk Dad keeps on buying. He seems to have gotten worse since Mama died."

"He took her death pretty hard." Arlene slowly shook her head. "Dad's always been a hoarder, but I believe he has more collections now than ever before. Larry says Dad has so many old milk cans sitting around the place he could start his own dairy. I enjoy going to yard sales, but only to look for practical things."

"And what about his collection of pens? I discovered two drawers in the kitchen desk, full of pens with different logos on them." Elsie rolled her eyes. "It's probably not the only place he's stashed his collection of pens, either. Due to the money Dad's gotten from the oil wells on his land, some people in our community have begun teasing him about being 'The Amish Millionaire.' Pretty soon, they'll be calling him 'The Eccentric Millionaire.'"

Arlene chuckled. "Guess what Aunt Verna told me once."

"About Dad?"

"*Jah.* She said even when he was a little guy he hoarded things. Since she's ten years older than Dad, I'm sure she remembers many of the things he did as a child."

"Did she say what kind of things he hoarded?"

"Not really. But she explained how he used to cry whenever their *mamm* threw anything out. He wanted to save everything."

"That's interesting. I'll have to ask Aunt Verna for more details the next time she comes for a visit."

Arlene's lips compressed. "Please don't ask her in front of Dad. He wouldn't take too kindly to us talking about his strange habits."

"You're right, but then maybe he thinks there's nothing odd about his habits. He might believe his actions are normal and we're being too scrutinizing of his ways. Anyway, while we're on the subject of our *daed*, what would you think about the two of us taking him out for lunch sometime soon? He enjoys eating at Der Dutchman in Walnut Creek, and we'll make sure Doris is working the day we go, so we can say hello to her, too."

Arlene nodded. "Good idea. Whoever sees Dad first can ask if he'd like to go."

Farmerstown, Ohio

"How's our little fellow doing?" Arlene asked her twelve-year-old daughter, Martha, when she returned home later in the afternoon.

Martha motioned to her four-month-old brother sleeping contentedly in his crib. "Samuel did well. When I was busy doing other things, Lillian kept him entertained." She spoke softly.

"Good to hear," Arlene whispered. "Did you both get your rooms cleaned like I asked?"

"Mine's all done. Lillian's upstairs finishing hers."

"I'm glad, because it'll be time to start supper soon, and I'll need both of you in the kitchen to help."

"How'd it go at Aunt Elsie's?" Martha asked after they'd left the baby's room.

"It went well. We got lots of beets canned, and some corn frozen, too. Elsie will be coming to help me tomorrow."

"Do English people help their family members as much as we Amish do?" Martha blinked her brown eyes.

Arlene shrugged. "I'm sure many of them do."

Martha gave her mother a hug. "I'm glad to be part of a family that cares about each other."

She gently patted her daughter's back. *Unfortunately, one of our family members doesn't seem to care much about anyone but himself.* Arlene did not voice her thought.

The distinctive *clip-clop* of horse's hooves coming up the driveway could be heard. Martha rushed to the kitchen window. "It's Grandpa's rig, Mom. Is he comin' for supper?"

"I wasn't expecting him," Arlene replied, "but he's always welcome, so we'll invite him to stay."

"I'll go help him put his horse away." Martha hurried out the door.

Arlene smiled. Her oldest daughter had always been helpful. Martha was also quite fond of her grandfather. Perhaps it was because they had something in common. Like him, Martha enjoyed collecting unusual things. Since Arlene's father lived nearby, they got to see him fairly often; whereas her husband, Larry's, parents lived in Wisconsin and the children weren't able to see them as much.

Arlene opened the refrigerator and took out the chicken she planned to fix for supper. She'd finished cutting it up when Dad entered the house with Martha.

"I have something for the *boppli*," he announced, grinning. "It's a wooden rocking horse I got at the auction today. I left it sitting in the utility room." He removed his straw hat, revealing a crop of thick brown hair with a few streaks of gray. If it weren't for Dad's full gray beard, no one would have guessed he was sixty-five years old.

"*Danki.* I appreciate the gift for the baby." Arlene moved toward him. "Where's the greeting you give whenever we see each other?"

Dad held out his arms. Arlene dried her hands on a paper towel and stepped into his embrace. It felt good to be hugged by her father. Dad's hugs were sincere, and Arlene always felt she was loved. She was certain he loved all four of his children, but Dad often said he felt closer to his three girls. Most likely it was because they all lived close, and he got to see them on a regular basis. Their brother, on the other hand, rarely came around.

Smiling, Arlene clutched Dad's arm. "I

saw Elsie earlier today. We were wondering if you'd like to go out to lunch with us—maybe one day next week."

"Sounds good to me." He hung his hat on the wall peg nearest him. "Where do ya want to go?"

"How about Der Dutchman? Since Doris works there, we'll get to see her, too—at least for a little while."

"Name the day. I'll be ready to go." Dad turned and tweaked Martha's upturned nose. "I'll bet you'd like to go, too, wouldn't ya?"

Martha nodded. "But someone will have to babysit Samuel, so I'll probably stay home. Besides, you and your *dochders* deserve some time together without the grandkids hanging around."

Dad peered at Arlene over the top of his glasses. "This girl's a *schmaert* one, just like her mamm."

Arlene smiled in response. "I'm frying chicken for supper, Dad. Would you like to stay and eat with us?"

"Sure would." Dad shuffled across the room and took a seat at the table. "Mind if I sit here and watch you cook? When your mamm was alive I used to keep her company in the kitchen whenever I could." He thumped his belly a couple of times. "Smellin' all the good food helped me work up a voracious appetite."

"What's that word mean?" Martha asked.

"It means 'greedy or ravenous.'"

Martha snickered, draping her arms around his chest from behind the chair he sat on. "I love you, Grandpa."

"That goes double for me." Grinning, he reached up and patted her hand.

"Would you like something to drink, Dad?" Arlene asked.

"Got any sweet tea in the refrigerator?"

"Sure do."

"I'll get you a glass, Grandpa." Martha went to get the beverage. When she returned, she placed it in front of him. "I put in some extra ice to help you cool off."

"Danki, that was thoughtful of you." Dad's face sobered, and the wrinkles around his brown eyes deepened. "Saw our bishop at the auction today. He thinks I oughta look for another *fraa*. Even said a few of the widows in the area might be interested in me."

"How do you feel about that?" Arlene asked, already sure of the answer.

He grunted and shook his head. "Don't need another wife. I told the bishop so, too. I'm gettin' along adequately on my own. Besides, no other woman could ever fill your mamm's shoes. My Effie was one in a million. She will always remain my fraa." As if the matter was entirely settled, Dad picked up the newspaper lying on his end of the table and snapped it open.

Arlene looked at her daughter and smiled. The whole family knew he had a stubborn streak. If Dad didn't want another wife, it didn't matter how many widows in their community were interested in him. Unless someone really special came along to change his mind, he'd no doubt remain single for the rest of his life.

Akron

Holding a glass of orange juice, Joel sank onto his couch with a groan. Lemonade would have tasted better, but orange juice was all he had in the refrigerator right now. At least it was cold. Joel had done a small job today on his own, knowing he couldn't pay anyone to help him right now. For that matter, he'd been trying to dodge several of his subcontractors all day. One he'd seen at the parts store. Another had called, asking for his money. A third man, who did the electrical work for most of Joel's jobs, had shown up at the house he'd been working on this morning, demanding his money. Joel told each of them the same thing: "I'm a little short on funds right now, but I'll get you paid as soon as I can."

Joel would keep his feelers out. He'd need a lot of jobs to get through the mess he'd gotten himself into. Usually he was asleep before his head hit the pillow, but Joel had a hard time getting to sleep last night due to his circumstances.

He rubbed his sweaty forehead. Right now, he felt like a defenseless cat being chased by an angry dog. It was his own fault for spending money he should have used to pay the people he owed. But the mistake had been made, and he wasn't about to give up the car—if he could even find a buyer with that kind of money.

Sweat rolled down Joel's temples as he glanced at the air conditioner he'd placed in the living-room window to help beat the heat. One lousy little unit wasn't enough to cool his single-wide, even if his home was small. If the weather cooled later, maybe he would sleep outside tonight.

I can't wait till I have enough money to build a new house. Sure can't marry Kristi and expect her to live in these cramped quarters, either. She deserves better than this.

Joel's cell phone rang. He pulled it out of his pocket to check the caller I.D. "Wish I could hide myself or become invisible until I have the money I need to right my debts," he muttered. Seeing the caller's name, he realized it was Rick, the plumber who usually worked for him. He probably wanted his money, too. Ignoring the call, Joel let his voice mail kick in. He couldn't deal with this right now. If he didn't get another big job quickly, he may have to do something drastic.

CHAPTER 5

Walnut Creek

On Monday of the following week, Joel had finished a small job at a residence in Zoar and was now approaching Walnut Creek to take a look at another possible job. Unfortunately, neither would bring in a lot of money.

Think I'll stop at Rebecca's Bistro and get something to eat, he decided. After the thirty-minute drive, Joel was even hungrier than before and ready to relax for a spell. He'd eaten at Rebecca's before, and the food had always been good, so he looked forward to it.

As Joel drew close to the small restaurant, he saw the parking lot was completely full. The long line of people standing at the entrance meant only one thing: it would be awhile until he got seated.

Oh, great! Joel's stomach rumbled in protest. Since he didn't have time to wait and was getting hungrier by the minute, he pulled his truck into Der Dutchman's parking lot. It was a bigger restaurant, and he could probably get in and out in half the time.

When Joel entered the building he was

taken to a seat near the windows. "Your waitress will be with you soon." As the hostess handed Joel a menu, his stomach growled once again. Embarrassed, he mumbled, "Sorry. Guess my belly is screaming to be fed."

She grinned at him. "It's okay. You're in the right place to take care of that."

Joel nodded and picked up his cell phone, figuring he may as well check his messages while he waited. The only one he found was from Kristi, asking if he'd like to go for a run with her after work this afternoon. Some exercise might help relieve some of the stress Joel felt, but it would do nothing to earn the money he needed. Even gazing at the beautiful car parked in his shop did little to ease his troubled mind.

Joel slipped his cell phone back in his pocket. *If Kristi knew what I was planning to do when I get back to Akron, she wouldn't want to go anywhere with me. Sure wish I didn't have to do this, but I don't see any other way.*

"Joel?"

He jerked his head, surprised to see his youngest sister standing beside his table. "Doris, what are you doing here?"

"I'm a waitress at this restaurant."

"Oh, I see. I. . .uh. . .didn't realize you worked here." Joel glanced down at his menu.

Wish now I'd waited in line at Rebecca's Bistro.
Doris was two years older than Joel, and they'd
been close when they were kids. But once
they'd become teenagers, she'd disapproved
of everything he did. Doris had lectured him
more often than either of his other sisters. Joel
hoped Doris wouldn't start in on him now.
If she did, he'd get up and walk out.

"How have you been, Joel?" she asked.

"Doin' okay." No way would he admit the
financial mess he was in. It would only open
the door for Doris to berate him about going
English. "How 'bout you? Everything goin'
okay in your life?"

She nodded, although not a hint of a smile
showed on her face. Was she angry at him for
leaving home, or perhaps still grieving Mom's
death? Maybe something else was going on
in her life.

"Aren't you going to ask how Dad and the
rest of the family are doing?" she questioned.

Joel's face heated. "Umm. . .you haven't
given me much of a chance to ask. So how is
everyone getting along these days?"

"As well as can be expected. We all miss
you. Are you too busy to drop by once in a
while, or are you deliberately staying away?"

Joel grimaced. *Here we go with the lecture.*
"This is not the time or place to be talking

about this. Now if you don't mind, I'd like something to eat. My stomach's about to jump out of my throat."

"Certainly. I see your appetite hasn't changed, at least. What would you like to have?"

Ignoring her sarcasm, Joel pointed to the menu. "I'll have a roast turkey sandwich with fries. Oh, and a glass of chocolate milk would be nice."

"I'll get your order turned in right away." Doris paused, moving closer to the table. "Why don't you come by for supper one night next week? I can make your favorite, hamburger and fries. In fact, we can do it picnic-style and get out the grill. I'll invite the rest of the family. I'm sure they'd all like to see you."

Joel folded his arms. "Yeah, I'll bet—especially Dad." It was hard to turn down a grilled burger, but he wasn't ready to face his entire family and be the focus of a thousand questions or the looks of irritation Dad often gave whenever Joel came around.

She frowned. "Don't be sarcastic, Joel. Dad may not say it, but he misses you, and so do the rest of us."

"The last time I visited, Dad didn't say more than a few words to me. Does snubbing me sound like someone who misses his only son?"

"I shouldn't need to remind you that our daed is a man of few words."

Joel shrugged. "If you say so."

"Will you come to supper or not?"

He shook his head. "I have a lot of work-related things going on right now. Maybe some other time."

Doris sighed. "I'll be back when your order is ready."

Joel blew out his breath, wishing once again he had picked another restaurant.

Joel had no more than finished his meal when he caught sight of a horse and buggy pulling into the section of the parking lot reserved for the Amish. That in itself was no surprise, since many Amish people patronized Der Dutchman. What surprised Joel was seeing who got out of the buggy. He grimaced as he watched his older sisters, Arlene and Elsie, accompanied by Dad, heading for the restaurant.

Quickly, Joel grabbed his bill and rushed over to the cash register. While it might not be right to avoid them, he wasn't in the mood for his sisters' questions or Dad's cold shoulder. After he'd paid for his meal, Joel realized if he went out the door right now he'd probably run head-on into his family. Rather than risk an encounter, he ducked into the restroom. He'd wait there until he was sure they'd been seated.

As Joel stood at the sink, combing his hair, he thought about the last time he and Dad talked. It had been awkward, and there really hadn't been much to say. Joel asked how Dad was doing, and Dad mumbled, "About the same." Joel asked if Dad could spare five hundred dollars, and Dad had given it to him, but not without a lecture. Of course, Joel was used to that. He'd had plenty of lectures from Dad during his teenaged years. "Don't stay out too late." "You don't need an expensive car." "You're full of *hochmut*, and pride goes before a fall." Joel had heard it all.

If Dad saw me driving the Corvette, he'd really believe I was full of pride. Well, it doesn't matter. I deserve that car. I've waited a long time to get one like it.

Thinking he'd given his family enough time to get seated, Joel opened the restroom door and peered out. No Amish in sight. He glanced toward the dining room and saw them seated at a table near the window, not far from where he'd been a short time ago. Relieved, he made a hasty exit. It was bad enough he'd seen Doris; Joel didn't need to deal with Dad, too.

As soon as Elsie entered the restaurant in Walnut Creek with Arlene and their father, she spotted their younger sister, Doris. "Let's ask the hostess to seat us in Doris's section," she whispered to Arlene.

"Okay, but we'd better not take up too much of her time visiting. We wouldn't want to jeopardize her job."

"Doris is too schmaert for that," Dad spoke up. "She knows better than to carry on a symposium all day with the customers when she oughta be tendin' to business."

Elsie looked at Arlene and rolled her eyes. Their father had always been right to the point and never minced any words—even the big ones, which had become his trait.

Soon after they were seated at a table, Doris showed up to take their order. "This is a pleasant surprise." She gave them each a glass of water. "Seeing my *schweschdere*, daed, and *bruder* all in the same day—what more could I ask for?"

Dad's eyebrows shot up. "Joel was here?"

Doris nodded. "You missed him by five minutes or so."

"Did he come in to see you?" Arlene asked.

"No, he didn't even realize I was working here until I came up to his table to wait on him."

"Humph! Bet you surprised him," Dad muttered.

"What did our bruder have to say?" Elsie questioned.

"Not much." Doris frowned. "I asked Joel if he'd like to come to our place for supper next week, but he used being too busy as an excuse. I even offered to make his favorite meal, but it didn't seem to matter."

Deep wrinkles formed across Dad's forehead as he pulled his fingers through the ends of his beard. "Sounds like he's using the same old excuse, but the truth is, he never comes around unless he wants something." He tapped his thumb on the menu. "Let's place our orders and forget about your wayward bruder. I'm *hungerich*, and Doris needs to put in our orders."

Saying anything more about Joel would get them nowhere, so Elsie kept quiet. The mention of their brother was a touchy subject where Dad was concerned. It had been this way ever since Joel left the Amish church and walked away from his family in search of what he thought was a better life. Quickly scanning her menu, she looked up at Doris and suggested, "Why don't you start with Dad? He probably knows what he wants already."

"Not really." Dad shook his head. "I can't decide between a hot dog and french fries, or the grilled cheese sandwich, also with fries."

"A hot dog's not very healthy, Dad." Doris pointed to the menu. "Why don't you have a roast turkey sandwich and a cup of soup?"

He scrunched up his nose. "No one can make a turkey sandwich the way your mamm does. I'll stick with a hot dog."

Elsie glanced at Arlene, sitting beside her. *Is she thinking what I'm thinking? Why does Dad sometimes talk about Mama as if she's still alive? Does he forget occasionally, or is it simply his way of coping with her death?*

Arlene merely looked at Doris and said, "I'd like the strawberry crunch salad and a cup of vegetable soup."

"What about you, Elsie?" Doris held her pencil above the ordering pad.

Elsie scanned the menu one more time. "I'll have the soup and salad bar. I like a nice variety of veggies to choose from."

Dad let out an undignified snort. "You girls and your salads. You need a little meat to put on your emaciated bones."

Elsie's forehead wrinkled. She wished her father didn't use big words so often. "Our what?"

"Emaciated bones. The word means, 'skinny.'" He pointed at Arlene. "Especially you, Daughter. You've gotten way too thin since the boppli was born."

Elsie held her breath, waiting to see how her sister would respond, but Arlene merely picked up her glass of water and took a drink.

Some things are better left unspoken, Elsie thought. *Especially when it comes to knowing when or how to give a reply to something Dad has said.*

"Do any of you want anything other than water to drink?" Doris asked.

Arlene and Elsie both shook their heads, but Dad was quick to say he wanted a glass of buttermilk. While some might find it strange to drink buttermilk with a hot dog, it was not uncommon for Dad. In fact, he had buttermilk with at least one of his meals every day. He'd been drinking it ever since Elsie could remember. Their mother had drunk it, too, but not as much as Dad. In fact, Mama made buttermilk biscuits and pancakes, which tasted so good. Elsie's mouth watered, thinking about it. She missed those days when her mother and father were together. Mama had always kept Dad in good spirits with her heartfelt humor and gentle ways. She had known how to soften his temper and keep him moving in a positive direction. Now it was up to Doris, Arlene, and Elsie to look after Dad. Joel sure wasn't going to help with that.

"I'll put in your orders and be back soon with your buttermilk." Doris smiled at Dad and hurried from the table.

"She looks thin, too," Dad commented. "Bet she eats like a bird. Your mamm was a well-built woman. She was perfect for me." He stared off into space and grunted. "My girls are just as pretty, though. They also attend church regularly and do well by their family, as well as others, which is more than I can say for that wayward son of mine." Dad's closed fist thumped the table. "Joel is spoiled by his wants and neglects those who should matter the most to him. He's pushed his family aside and forgotten his Amish upbringing." He sat back in his chair and slid his feet noisily forward under the table, the way he often did at home when he was upset.

Elsie's shoulders slumped as she let out a soft breath. She didn't remember her father being so critical when Mama was alive. Could he be this way because he missed her so much and felt depressed? She couldn't really blame him. But life moved on, and she hoped he would find some happiness.

Wanting to talk about something else, Elsie looked out the window and pointed to the vivid blue sky. "Sure is a beautiful day. Not nearly as much humidity as last week."

"I know. The weather was miserable, but it's good we got the canning done when we did." Arlene smiled at Dad. "I'll bring you some pickled beets soon. Would you like some?"

He smacked his lips. "Sounds *wunderbaar*!"

Elsie relaxed in her chair. At least the mention of beets had put Dad on a positive note. Now to keep things upbeat throughout the rest of their meal.

CHAPTER 6

Akron

Kristi turned on the coffeemaker and fixed herself a piece of toast. She'd forgotten to set her alarm last night, but fortunately, the early morning light had awakened her. She still had several minutes to spare.

The aroma of freshly brewed coffee drew Kristi to her kitchen for that first cup. Coffee wasn't on her ideal drink list, but she made an exception for her morning brew to get a kick-start to her Friday morning.

As Kristi sat at the table eating her low-calorie breakfast, she thought about Joel, and how, when they'd gone jogging last night, he'd acted strange—almost as if he was hiding something.

But what could it be? She reached for the jar of sugar-free strawberry jelly to put on her toast. *It was probably my imagination. He may have been tired.* Kristi's gaze fixated on her cup, watching the delicate swirl of steam rise from the surface of the coffee. She had a habit of over-analyzing things, especially where Joel was concerned. He had a business to run, which had to be stressful at times. Joel had a right to act sullen or moody when his day wasn't going as planned. Kristi hoped once they were married, Joel wouldn't let his business affect their relationship. *If we ever get married. Joel still hasn't bought me an engagement ring or suggested setting a wedding date. I don't want to push him, but I wish he'd at least introduce me to his family.*

It wasn't fair. Joel had met Kristi's family, but she hadn't met his. Every time the topic came up, Joel either changed the subject or said she wouldn't fit in with his family, and for that matter, neither did he. Kristi figured he must have had a falling out with someone to be so dead set against her meeting them. She would have to be patient where his family was concerned. Maybe by the time she and Joel set a wedding date, he'd be ready to introduce her to them.

Kristi glanced at her watch, then gulped down the rest of her coffee. She needed to make a sandwich for lunch and get out the door soon or she'd be late for work.

Charm, Ohio

Eustace Byler stood on his porch, gazing at the trees lining the back of his property. The smell of pine filled the morning air, and it seemed to melt his tensions away. Listening to the birds singing brought his thoughts to a sweeter time when his wife, Effie, used to say he ought to build a tree house so they could see things from the birds' perspective. Eustace kept promising to construct the little house in the trees, but had never gotten around to it. The plans had been drawn up, but getting started seemed to be the hard part. Other things seemed more urgent.

During the summer months, Effie spent time nearly every day relaxing in her favorite chair on the front porch with a cup of tea. She'd loved watching the birds and kept several feeders filled with a variety of seeds to lure them in. She would often comment on the birds' activity, listening to the steady chatter in undeniable disagreements as they competed for the best spot to perch. Effie used to say the birds were free entertainment at all times of the year.

Eustace groaned. "Why'd your heart have to give out on you, Effie? Don't ya know how much I still need you here by my side?" Someday he would build the tree house in memory of Effie. Then every time he went up there, he'd be reminded of his dear, loving wife.

Eustace's stomach growled, reminding

him that he hadn't had breakfast yet. Turning toward the house, he went inside and made his way to the kitchen. When his gaze came to rest on the gas stove, he was reminded once again how much he missed his wife. When she was alive, Eustace would come inside after doing his chores and could always count on Effie having breakfast waiting for him. The wonderful aromas of whatever she prepared would reach his nostrils before he got to the door. Now he had to fend for himself. Since he wasn't the best cook in Holmes County, he usually ended up eating cold cereal or a piece of bread with peanut butter for breakfast. This morning, however, Eustace had a craving for steak and eggs. *I'll cook the steak on the grill.*

Eustace set the frying pan on the stove; took a carton of eggs, some ketchup, and the steak from the refrigerator; and went back outside. After he poured several briquettes into the bottom of the grill, he squirted lighter fluid over them and lit a match. Nothing happened. He added more fluid, lit a second match, and tossed it in.

Whoosh! The flames shot up. Eustace jumped back, but not soon enough. The sulfur-like smell could only mean one thing: he'd singed his beard. To make sure the fire was out, he picked up the potholder he kept on the porch table and smacked at his beard several times. Then, placing the steak on the grill, he went back inside to check on the damage he'd done.

One look in the bathroom mirror and Eustace realized his beard was more than half the length it had once been. To make matters worse, the singed ends were dark. He opened the medicine chest and took out a pair of scissors. He had no choice but to trim off the scorched part, which made his beard even shorter.

"I'll probably be bombarded with all sorts of questions about this," Eustace grumbled, heading back outside to tend the meat. "Shoulda fixed a bowl of cereal instead of tryin' to satisfy my craving for steak and eggs."

Akron

Even though the cool morning air was invigorating, Joel's jumbled thoughts made it hard to concentrate as he drove his work truck to town. He had been so preoccupied that he'd forgotten to fill his rig with gas last evening before heading home. Now the fuel gage sat on empty. He didn't need this headache on top of everything else.

Sweat beaded on Joel's forehead, but not from the outside temperatures. He hoped there was enough gas in his truck to get to town. He'd ridden on fumes a few times before, so maybe this time would be no different.

In an effort not to be consumed by his anxiety about the gas, Joel concentrated on what he was about to do. He'd convinced himself that taking money from his and Kristi's bank account was the right thing, but his conscience told him otherwise, constantly reminding him that the position he'd put himself in was his own fault. He'd never been one to admit his mistakes, however. Even when he was a young boy, it had been easier to wangle his way out of things rather than face the truth and admit he was wrong. He had come up with an idea to fix the mess he was in, and right or wrong, he'd carry out the plan.

Joel had gotten back too late yesterday to make it to the bank, which had given him more time to think things through. But it hadn't helped much, because after looking at his last bank statement, he realized the money in their joint account would only pay a few of his subcontractors. He didn't dare draw it all out, either. Thank goodness the monthly statements came to his place and not Kristi's.

The last thing he needed was for her to find out he'd taken the money without her knowledge.

Joel swiped at the sweat on his forehead as he approached the bank. The gas station, which wasn't too far away, would be his next stop. With the exception of not telling Kristi about his family, he'd never done anything this deceitful to her. But he couldn't come right out and ask if she minded if he borrowed their money to pay his debts; he'd then have to tell her about the Corvette.

I can't worry about it right now, he thought, stepping into the bank. *I need to solve this problem.*

When Joel left the bank, he squinted against the glare of the sun. In his hurry to leave this morning, he'd forgotten his sunglasses.

Climbing back into the truck, Joel felt a headache coming on. Was it from the glare on his windshield, or the stress of what he'd just done?

"I'm really in a pickle right now," he muttered. The sun's brightness and his near-empty fuel tank were just a small part of the bigger frustrations plaguing him. All Joel could really hope for was that another big job would come along so he could pay the rest of his men, plus have enough to put back in the bank what he'd withdrawn. If things didn't go his way soon, he may have no other option but to make a trip to see his dad. But that was the last thing he wanted to do.

CHAPTER 7

After a week with only small job prospects, Joel had no choice but to visit his father and ask for a loan. He was almost out the door when his cell phone rang. As soon as he realized it was Kristi, he answered. "Hey, Kristi, what's up?"

"I was wondering if you'd like to go for another run with me this evening."

"Uh. . .I can't do it today."

"How come?"

"I have to go out of town on business, and I'm not sure what time I'll get home. It'll probably be late."

"Oh, I see. Maybe tomorrow then? Since it's Saturday, I'll have the day off."

"Sure, that'll be fine." Joel shifted the phone to his other ear. "Listen, I'd better go. I'll see you tomorrow, Kristi."

"Okay. I hope you have a good day."

"You too." Joel hesitated a minute, then quickly added, "Love you." Before Kristi could respond, he clicked off his phone, grabbed his truck keys and sunglasses, and headed out the door.

Joel made a face when he glanced at his truck. The outside was a mess and needed a good washing. At least he'd taken the time to clean the windshield. Joel wished he could drive the Corvette to Charm, if for no other reason than to see how it performed once again on the open road. But he couldn't show up with an expensive car and then ask for money to help him out of a jam. Joel hoped his dad would be glad to see him and have no problem opening his wallet.

As Joel stepped into his truck, he reflected on the lie he'd told Kristi about where he was going today. It really wasn't a lie. He technically would be out of town doing business— with his dad. It was either tell a fib or tell Kristi the truth, which he definitely did not want to do. *I may never be ready to tell her about my Amish family,* he thought. *Then I'd have to explain the reasons I left and admit I used to be engaged to someone else.*

Over and over, Joel contemplated how he could tell Kristi about his past, but he found no easy way to announce that he used to be Amish. One thing was certain: Joel would avoid it for as long as possible—maybe indefinitely. If only Dad would give him the money. What a relief it would be to replace what he took out of the bank and be able to pay off his debts. Hopefully by tomorrow, things would be as they should.

Charm

As Eustace headed to the barn to let the horses into the pasture, he heard the soft cooing of doves, which made him think once again about Effie. Everything around here brought some sort of memory about his wife—the flowers blooming in late August, the birds singing overhead.

Unbidden tears sprang to Eustace's eyes, remembering how, whenever he used to bring the horses in for the night, he'd see Effie waiting on the porch, waving at him. He would remove his straw hat and wave in response. Eustace always drew comfort in knowing Effie would be there to greet him after his chores were done.

It had been a week since he'd singed his beard, and of course, he'd received some comments from family members, as well as friends at church on Sunday, which was embarrassing. Especially the part about how it happened. Now he had to be patient while it grew back.

I wonder if I combed or brushed my beard a lot more if it might help it grow faster, he mused. *Or maybe there's some kind of lotion I could look for at the drugstore that would quicken the process.* Eustace shook his head. *Guess it's probably best*

to leave it alone and let time take care of things.
Eustace's friend Henry hadn't seen his beard
yet, but he was due here anytime, so Eustace
was prepared for some ribbing.

Entering the barn, Eustace thought about
Joel, and how, as a boy, he'd helped bring in
and let out the horses every day. Never in
all of Joel's years of growing up had Eustace
suspected his son would become dissatisfied
with the only life he'd ever known. He'd
seemed content when he was a boy. Eustace
had foolishly convinced himself Joel would
someday follow in his footsteps and raise
horses, the way he had before he'd agreed to
let oil wells be placed on his property. Now
that money was no object, Eustace only raised
a few horses for his own enjoyment.

"I was sure wrong about my boy. Guess I
didn't know him as well as I thought." Eustace
yanked off his old straw hat and swatted
one of the horses to get her moving. In his
exuberance, he missed the critter's rump and
hit the side of the barn instead.

"Oh, great. Not what I needed this morning." Eustace squinted at the brim of his
hat where a chunk had broken off. "Guess I
deserve it for not payin' attention to what I
was doing."

Once the horses were out, Eustace went

back in the house. Grunting, he plunked down in his favorite chair with wheels, rolled over to his desk, and pulled the junk drawer open. After removing the roll of duct tape, he proceeded to tape the brim back on his hat.

Effie had bought the hat for him two years before she died, so he wasn't about to throw it out. The only sensible thing to do was mend it the best way he could. If it looked ridiculous, then, oh well! He'd only be wearing it for everyday, so it didn't matter what others might say.

Rolling his chair back across the room, Eustace pulled up to the table and grabbed a banana to tide him over until lunchtime. Rising from his seat, he ambled over to the refrigerator. *Think I'll have a glass of buttermilk to go with the banana. Then I need to go over the plans one more time before I start working on the tree house.*

While getting out the milk, Eustace heard the familiar rumble of a tractor coming up the drive. He knew without looking it was his New Order Amish friend, Henry Raber. Old Henry rode around in that tractor more than his horse and buggy.

Eustace went out the door, leaving his glass of buttermilk on the counter. As soon as he stepped onto the porch he heard Henry's dog, Peaches, howling like a baby from her metal carrier fastened to the back of the tractor. Peaches, so named for the color of her hair, was always with Henry whenever he came to visit. The cocker spaniel was kind of cute, but she was a fat little thing with a hearty set of lungs.

"Morning, Henry," Eustace called. "Glad ya came by. How's everything with you these days?"

"Can't complain I—" Henry tipped his head. "Say, what happened to your beard?"

Eustace groaned, reaching up to touch his shorter chin hairs. "Got a little too close to the barbecue grill when the flames shot up." He went on to tell his friend the rest of the story.

With a snicker, Henry thumped Eustace's back. "You're lucky ya didn't lose your whole beard."

Eustace nodded. "Indubitably."

"Indu-what?" Henry's brows squeezed together.

"Indubitably. It means 'definitely.'"

"Sounds like you've had your nose in the dictionary again."

"Yep. It's a great pastime, and I learn a lot." Eustace clasped his friend's shoulder. "So what have you been up to so far today?"

"Saw the widow-woman Ida at the post office this morning. She asked how you were doing." Chuckling, Henry yanked on his full gray beard and nodded. "Jah, she was anxious to know that, alright."

"So what'd ya tell her?" Eustace leaned on the porch railing.

"Said as far I knew you were good and I was heading out to see you." Henry walked up to the carrier to let his faithful companion out. The dog looked at Henry and tipped her head. *Yip! Yip!*

"Alright, already." Henry leaned down and, as if in slow-motion, lifted Peaches into his arms. One thing about old Henry—he did things slowly, never in much of a hurry.

"Well, that widow-woman may be interested in me," Eustace commented, "but my heart will never belong to anyone but dear Effie. Now enough talk about Ida. Let's go inside, and I'll get some coffee brewing. Oh, and I've got some blueberry fry pies to go with it that my daughter Doris picked up at Der Dutchman Bakery yesterday. She works next door in the restaurant, ya know."

Henry bobbed his graying head. "She's waited on me a time or two. You have a thoughtful dochder, Eustace."

"Jah. Doris sometimes brings me a sandwich

or soup for supper." Eustace smiled. "All three of my daughters go out of their way to help out. They always want to clean around here or just drop by to check up on me, no matter how much resisting I do."

Henry thumped Eustace's back. "I, myself, would be in favor of all that fussin'. But then, you aren't like me."

"That's true. We're different, alright, but still good friends."

Henry took a seat at the table, still holding Peaches like she was his baby. "With most of my *kinner* in Indiana, I get far less attention than you do." He scratched Peaches behind her left ear. "But I'm content with what I've got."

Taking a sip from his glass of buttermilk, Eustace nodded. "I like to do things my own way. If I wanna climb a tree and cut off branches, I do it. No one likes to be told to wait on someone else to help when they can do it themselves." He puffed out his chest. "I may be sixty-five, but I'm more than capable of doing most chores around here myself. In fact, I'm quite proficient. Besides, I enjoy the work. Keeps me from missin' Effie so much. I can't stand to be idle." Eustace moved across the room. "Guess I'd better get the coffee goin'."

Berlin

"I'm going out to check for phone messages," Elsie called to her fifteen-year-old daughter, Mary. "Will you keep an eye on the breakfast casserole I have in the oven?"

Mary's blue eyes twinkled as she bobbed her head. "Sure, Mom. Hope and I will also set the table."

Elsie smiled. "Danki." She appreciated her two girls and their willingness to help, even without being asked. "The casserole should be done by the time I come back to the kitchen, and then as soon as your daed and brothers finish up with their chores, we can eat."

"Good, 'cause I'm hungerich." Hope, who had recently turned eleven, spoke up.

Mary giggled and poked her sister's arm. "You're always hungry. You could probably eat more than both of our brothers put together."

Hope made no comment as she opened the cupboard door and took out six plates, placing them on the table. Elsie was pleased her youngest daughter could take a little joshing without getting upset. Some children, like her nephew Scott, became defensive when teased. He also had a bit of a temper, but Elsie's sister Arlene and her husband, Larry, had been working with Scott on the issue.

Elsie went out the back door. Stopping at her garden, she bent to pull a few weeds. If she didn't keep at them, they would soon choke out the plants. Things had been growing well this year. Vegetables were abundant, with plenty of tomatoes, green beans, corn, zucchini, and potatoes. After breakfast she would enlist the girls' help to pick and snap beans so they could have some for supper. She smiled, glancing at the carrots. They were sure getting bigger. This had been a great year for her garden.

Moving on down the driveway, Elsie opened the door to the phone shack to check for messages. She had no more than stepped inside when a spider web hit her in the face. "Eww..."

She cleaned the sticky web off her face and then checked her fingers, relieved there was no spider. From the time Elsie was a little girl, she'd had a spider phobia. Whenever she'd seen one, she had nearly freaked and usually asked someone to get rid of it for her. Since Elsie was now an adult, she took care of things like disposing of unwanted bugs, unless her husband was around of course.

Elsie took a seat in the folding chair, and was about to check the answering machine, when an ugly brown spider, hovering on a single web strand, lowered itself in front of her face. She screamed, ducked under the spider, and bolted out the door. Trembling, Elsie drew in a few shaky breaths. She had to go back in and check for messages, but not until the spider was out.

She spotted a twig lying in the yard and bent to pick it up. *I wish John or one of the kinner was here to do this for me right now,* she thought. *Since they're not, it won't get done unless I do it myself. I sure hope that spider is still there and not hiding in some corner waiting to creep me out again.*

Cautiously, Elsie stepped back into the phone shack. Sure enough, the spider was still there, dangling over the answering machine. Despite her trepidation, Elsie held out her hand, wrapping both spider and web around the twig. Then she carefully took the creature outside, placing it on a bush farther away. Once the job was done, she re-entered the phone shack and quickly checked for messages. The first was from her driver, saying she would be available Monday afternoon to take Elsie to her dental appointment. The second message surprised Elsie the most. It was from her brother, Joel, saying he'd be coming for a visit later this afternoon. It had been several months since they'd seen or heard from Joel. Elsie hoped this visit would go better than the last. Did she dare anticipate Joel may have decided to return to his Amish faith? Or was it wishful thinking? The fact of the matter hadn't changed—Dad was still hurt and angry because Joel turned his back on his family, as well as his faith. Deep down, however, Elsie felt sure Dad loved his son as much as his daughters.

Think I'll plan a big supper this evening and invite everyone over to Dad's place. I won't tell Dad, though. I want it to be a surprise.

CHAPTER 8

Charm

Joel pulled his truck off to the side of the road and got out. As he leaned against the door and closed his eyes, familiar sounds came to his ears. The dog days of summer had definitely arrived, and it was anything but silent in late August. Instead of hearing the birds' constant melodies, he picked up the sound of certain bugs singing their own tunes. Crickets chirped, cicadas buzzed, and locust sounds were at their peak. *Trrrrrr. . . c-c-c-c. . .*

Memories from Joel's childhood flooded his mind as he stood on the hill above his father's house and looked down. He remembered many afternoons on this very rise, lying on his back, watching the clouds while enjoying the noises surrounding him.

A small grin reached Joel's lips as he wondered how, after all these years, a chorus of bugs could remind him of school days starting soon.

Joel could see the old swing hanging from the big maple tree, still looking as it had when he was a boy. He and Doris, being the youngest siblings and closest in age, had taken turns pushing each other on the swing a good many times. They'd run through the barn, chasing the cats, and climbed into the hayloft to daydream and talk about the future. Little had Joel known that he'd someday have his own business, let alone become part of the English world. It surprised him how content he was living a different way of life than his family assumed he would. At least Joel thought he was content. If he were completely honest, part of him still missed some aspects of being Amish, but he'd been English for seven years now. For the most part, it felt right. He was not about to give up the dream he was living, nor break up with Kristi. The Amish way had many good aspects, but it wasn't for Joel anymore.

Turning his back on the farm and surveying the land around it, Joel saw nothing much had changed. He walked over to an area still familiar to him. Except for the weeds encompassing the spot, the seat he had made by arranging two rocks remained in place since the day he'd put them there. This rock-seat, situated in front of a large oak up on the knoll, had always been a happy place—Joel's private spot.

He watched as several dragonflies hovered over the grasses and colorful butterflies flitted from one plant to another, trying to find the last of the late-summer blooms. Joel took a deep breath and ran his fingers through his hair. *If only life could be as simple.*

About to lower himself to the old familiar seat, Joel's head jerked at the sound of a horse and buggy. Turning, he saw it approach and then stop. A few seconds later, his sister Doris got out. "Elsie said you were coming, but I didn't believe her." She moved closer to Joel. "Dad's gonna be surprised you're here." She gave him an awkward hug; Joel felt the strain between them.

"Why would he be surprised?" He glanced down the hill at their father's place. "When I called Elsie, I asked her to let Dad know I was coming."

"Guess she figured it was best not to say anything." Doris looked toward the open buggy, where her husband, Brian, sat holding the reins; then she turned her gaze back to Joel. "Elsie invited all of us to Dad's for supper this evening. She thought he would enjoy having his whole family together again." She folded her arms. "It's been awhile, you know."

"I've been busy with my business."

She glared at him. "Nobody should be too busy for family, Joel. But then you've never gotten that or you wouldn't have left us in the first place. Not to mention how bad you hurt your *aldi*."

Joel held up his hand, defiance welling in his soul as he looked at her. "Let's not even go there, okay? The past is in the past, and there's no going back. I'm sure Anna Detweiler has moved on with her life by now."

"She's still teaching school and keeps busy with other things, but Anna has remained single and hasn't had a serious boyfriend since you broke up with her."

Joel grimaced. The reminder of what he'd done to Anna made his stomach tighten. He still wondered if he and Anna might be married by now if she had been willing to leave with him. *But then I would never have met Kristi,* he thought. *Anna and I had some problems, and I'm sure Kristi's the perfect girl for me.*

Joel's thoughts came to a halt when Doris touched his arm. "Are you ready to head down the hill to Dad's now? I see two buggies near his barn, so I'm sure the others are there already."

Joel gave a nod. What else could he do? He was here and needed to ask Dad for money. He wished his sisters hadn't come, though. It would be harder to speak to Dad with the others around.

Glancing at the farm once again, Joel

felt like an outsider. Even with all the good memories flooding back, he didn't feel as comfortable as he should be with family.

Akron

When Kristi wheeled Mildred Parker, one of her patients, into the social room at the nursing home where she worked, her attention was drawn to an elderly man sitting in an easy chair near the window. It wasn't his flowing white hair and long Santa Claus beard that caught her attention, however—it was the beautiful music coming from the harmonica he held between his lips.

Joel had a harmonica similar to the man's, but Kristi hadn't heard him play it for several weeks. He'd seemed so preoccupied lately. Whenever she talked to him, he didn't appear to be really listening. What Joel needed was to relax more and have some fun for a change. Having work on his mind all the time wasn't a good thing for Joel—or for their relationship.

I'll bet a trip to Amish country would help Joel relax. It sure did for me, Kristi mused. *I wish he was willing to go there with me. When I catch Joel in the right mood, I'll ask again.*

Smiling, Kristi parked Mildred's wheelchair near the man with the flowing beard and took a seat beside her patient to listen to the melodic sounds of "Amazing Grace." Several of the patients, as well as family members who had come to visit, joined in by singing the familiar hymn. The man playing the harmonica seemed not to notice, as he closed his eyes and lifted his gaze toward the ceiling. Perhaps it was his way of worshipping God. Hearing his song had certainly warmed Kristi's heart and put her in a worshipful frame of mind. It made her look forward to this coming Sunday, when she and Joel could attend church. It might be fun to plan a bicycle ride later in the afternoon. They could either take a picnic lunch along or stop at one of the local restaurants for a bite to eat. It would be fun to be together. Maybe she could talk Joel into bringing his harmonica.

As Kristi let the music envelope her thoughts, her gaze drifted to the window. When she'd first started working at the nursing home, she'd been told this room wasn't always so popular. Now it was a favorite with patients and visitors alike, in part because the view from the window had changed from plain old grass to a landscaped nature garden. Flowering shrubs and unusual rocks surrounded a fish pond. At the far end, facing the window, a small waterfall cascaded into the tranquil pool. Pink-and-white water lilies floated on top, with several koi fish peacefully swimming through the clear water. Their orange-and-white bodies created a sharp contrast to the brown river pebbles on the floor of the pond.

The social room, with the large picture window, was a nice place for the residents to relax and feel comfortable. It was peaceful, and the employees at the nursing home often visited the room during their breaks.

Kristi glanced at her watch. She needed to check on another patient before her shift ended for the day, so reluctantly, she turned from the window. Then, leaning over to tell Mildred she would be back for her soon, Kristi quietly left the room.

Charm

Joel parked his truck near the barn and got out. Looking around, it didn't take him long to realize that, with the exception of a few more old wagon wheels and several antique milk cans scattered around, the place hadn't changed much. Dad was a junk collector and always had been. But then, Joel had to admit, he had a few of his own things he couldn't part with. If he had the chance, he'd have a collection of classic cars—not sitting around the yard, of course. Some, he'd fix up and sell for a profit, but others he would keep for the pure pleasure of having them.

"Hey, Joel, it's good to see you. How have ya been?" Arlene's husband, Larry, asked as he headed for the barn with his horse.

"Okay, I guess." As Joel entered the barn behind his blond-haired brother-in-law, he winced at the putrid odor of horse urine and scowled at the cobwebs hanging from the rafters.

Larry stopped and looked back at him. "I'd say this barn could use a good cleaning."

"I agree. When I was a boy, Dad used to keep it much cleaner. Of course," Joel added, "I usually helped him with that. When was the last time Dad cleaned the barn anyway?"

Larry shrugged. "Brian, John, and I have offered to do it for him many times, but he always refuses our help."

Joel frowned. "Figures. He's as stubborn as ever."

The place was thick with flies. He swatted at a few as he watched Larry lead his horse into one of the empty stalls. When Joel's mother was alive, Dad always made sure either he or Joel kept the barn and other outbuildings clean and fresh, with plenty of fly strips hanging from the rafters to keep the pesky bugs at bay. Mom had even kept a lid on some of Dad's eccentricities, but no one was there to do that anymore.

Joel shook his head. *Dad shouldn't be living alone. I sure don't have the time or patience to take care of him, though. Besides, he wouldn't want to live in my fancy world. You'd think he'd move in with one of my sisters or, at the very least, hire someone to help out around here. With the oil fracking being done on Dad's property, it's not like he can't afford it. I'll bet he has more money than he knows what to do with.*

"So where's my dad?" Joel asked, leaning on the door of the horse's stall.

Larry shrugged. "Don't know. I'm guessin' he must be in the house. I'll bet he'll be glad to see you."

Joel opened his mouth, but as he was about to speak, he inhaled a fly and swallowed the filthy insect before it even registered what had happened. He coughed and sputtered, trying to get it back up, but it seemed to be lodged in his throat.

Dashing out of the barn, Joel flung his truck door open, grabbed a bottle of water, and took a big swig. "Life on the farm," he muttered. "Guess all the memories weren't so good."

"Uncle Joel!" Joel's nephew Scott bounded

up to him with a huge smile on his freckled face. "Are ya movin' in with Grandpa, or did ya come to ask him for somethin'?"

Joel's face heated. Apparently there'd been some talk among family members about him only coming around when he wanted something. *I don't care if they do talk behind my back.* Drawing in a quick breath, Joel collected himself to face his family. Then he gave Scott's shoulder a squeeze and pointed to the house. "I'm sure whatever my sisters have made for the meal will be good." He stepped onto the porch and took another deep breath. "Shall we go inside and see what's for supper?"

CHAPTER 9

When Joel entered the house with Scott at his side, he expected to see his father sitting in the living room in his favorite chair. What he saw instead was his sister Arlene sitting in Mom's rocking chair, holding a baby. Except for a few gray hairs mingled with strands of brown sticking out from under her white head covering, she looked the same as the last time he'd seen her.

Arlene looked up and smiled. "It's nice you came, Joel. Elsie and Doris are in the kitchen, and the menfolk and most of the kinner are in the basement looking at something Dad recently bought."

He gave a brief nod. Then giving the living room a quick scan, he noticed it hadn't changed at all. Every stick of furniture remained in its place. The braided throw rug Mom had made many years ago was missing, though. It had probably worn all the way through from Dad wheeling about the house in his favorite chair. The marks on the wooden floor told the story.

Glancing toward the kitchen, Joel heard his other two sisters speaking their traditional German-Dutch language. Even though he didn't use it anymore, Joel understood it all perfectly.

"I'd like you to meet your newest nephew, Samuel. He's four months old." When Joel looked back at Arlene, she motioned to the infant.

Joel looked at Scott, still standing beside him with a cheesy grin, then back at the baby, realizing the brothers were eight years apart. "I—I wasn't aware you'd had another child."

"If you came around once in a while, you'd realize what's going on in our family."

Joel jerked his head at the sound of his father's voice. Dad stood in the doorway between the living room and kitchen with his arms crossed over his chest. "What are you doing here, anyway?"

"I—I came to see you," Joel stammered, feeling like a kid again as his dad scrutinized him. "Figured Elsie would tell you I was coming."

"No, she didn't." When Dad pulled his fingers through his beard, Joel noticed it was much shorter than it had been before. He wondered what happened, but before he could ask, Arlene spoke up.

"We wanted your coming to be a surprise."

Dad tapped his foot, never taking his eyes off Joel. "It's a surprise, alright. Wasn't sure we'd ever see your wayward bruder again."

Joel clenched his fists. He didn't like the

way his dad was staring right at him while talking to Arlene like he wasn't even in the room.

Joel's brothers-in-law, John, Larry, and Brian, entered the room, along with Joel's nephews, Doug, Glen, and Blaine. They each took turns shaking Joel's hand. Their cordial welcome made Joel feel a little more relaxed. He was glad Scott had left to use the bathroom and hadn't heard Dad's caustic remarks.

A few seconds later, Doris and Elsie came in from the kitchen, along with Joel's nieces, Martha, Lillian, Mary, and Hope.

"Well, Joel is here now, Dad, so I think we should all eat and enjoy our time together." Arlene stood, and when Doris held her arms out, she handed the baby to her. Joel couldn't help but notice the look of longing on his youngest sister's face. No doubt she wanted a baby of her own.

Soon after, when Scott joined them in the dining room, the hot food was brought out and placed on the table. The aromas caused Joel's mouth to water. Elsie, her brown eyes appearing darker than usual, immediately stepped over to Joel and gave him a hug. "I'm glad we could all gather this way to catch up, like a real family."

When Joel stepped away from her embrace, he nodded.

"The food is ready." Elsie looked at Dad.

"Humph!" He shuffled across the room and took a seat at the head of the table.

Everyone gathered and found seats as well. Joel was relieved he hadn't been asked to sit at a separate table, the way he had when he'd first left the Amish faith and returned home for a meal. But Dad was as cool and unfriendly as ever. Scott, however, was all smiles when he took a seat to the left of Joel.

All heads bowed for silent prayer, which felt strange to Joel, since Kristi always prayed out loud. Joel didn't pray much anymore. He only went along with it for Kristi's sake. If he didn't go to church with her and appear to be interested in spiritual things, she'd probably break up with him. He would do whatever it took to hold on to Kristi and make sure she'd never leave him. They had a good relationship, and he wasn't about to let her go. Meeting Kristi was the best thing that had ever happened to Joel. *If she heard I was sitting here right now with my Amish family, she wouldn't believe it for a minute,* he mused.

Eustace sat across the table from Joel, longing for his son to sit at his table like the guest of honor tonight. Instead tension filled the room, like it always did when Joel came around.

Brian, Doris's husband, who sat on Joel's other side, leaned closer and asked, "How's the construction business going?"

Joel shifted in his chair; then clearing his throat, he drank some water. "Uh. . .well, my business has been doing fairly well. I have several jobs lined up right now." His cheeks reddened a bit. "How about you, Brian? How's the carpentry business?"

"Doin' good. I like my job." Brian bobbed his brown head. "My corn's growing well this year, too. Looks to be a great crop. It should yield us quite a bit this fall. Doris and I are hoping to save up enough money to take a trip together sometime next year." He leaned back in his chair and grinned at his wife. "We'd like to go to Florida—maybe in January or February—when the weather gets cold here."

Joel nodded briefly. He seemed preoccupied and a bit edgy. *I wonder if he's hiding something,* Eustace thought. *I can sense it in his tone and the way he avoids making eye contact with everyone.*

A muscle on the side of Eustace's neck quivered. Having Joel here was like a two-edged knife. While it was good to have the whole family together, it grieved Eustace to see his son sitting here in English clothes, barely saying a word to anyone unless he was asked a question. Others in their community had children who'd left the faith, but none acted as haughty and distant as Eustace's son. What had happened to make Joel become so dissatisfied? Had Eustace done something to turn his son away? If Effie were still alive, would she be able to talk their son into moving back home and joining the Amish church again? *Maybe not. Effie wasn't able to make Joel see reason before she died.* Eustace gripped the edge of the table. It had nearly broken poor Effie's heart when their youngest child left to go English.

I need to quit thinking about this, because, short of a miracle, my son will never return to our faith, Eustace told himself. *Joel only comes around when he wants something, and I'm sure it's no different this time. But I'm not going to let his being here spoil my supper.*

"Please pass me the mashed *grummbiere.*" Eustace reached out, looking at Elsie.

She smiled and handed him the bowl. "I fixed them the way Mama used to. Plenty of milk to make the potatoes creamy, and of course, salt and pepper."

Eustace plopped some on his plate, squeezed a bit of ketchup out of the bottle, and took a bite. "Not quite as favorable as your mamm's, but not so bad, either." He glanced at

Joel. "What do ya think of this fine meal set before you? Bet ya don't get food this exquisite anywhere in the English world."

Joel smiled, but the expression didn't quite reach his eyes. "Everything tastes great." He reached for a piece of chicken. "My sisters are the best cooks in all of Holmes County."

"Danki," Arlene and Elsie replied in unison, but Doris remained quiet. She hadn't said more than a few words since they sat down at the table.

It shouldn't be like this. Eustace slid his feet back and forth under the table. *There should be good feelings among everyone here at my table.* He wondered if Doris might still be angry at Joel for breaking up with her best friend, Anna, when he made the decision to go English and move to Akron in pursuit of worldly pleasures. Anna had been devastated by Joel's rejection, and like a good friend, Doris had been there to help her get through it.

Eustace felt bad about what Joel had put Anna through, but the main reason he wasn't happy to see Joel this evening had nothing to do with Joel's ex-girlfriend. Simply put, Eustace was almost sure Joel's only reason for coming here was to ask for money, like he had the last time he'd visited. Well, if that turned out to be the case, he'd be sorely disappointed.

As Doris ate her meal, she kept watching Joel. He hadn't contributed much to the conversation. The only time he ever smiled was when young Scott said something to him. Why did he bother to come here this evening if he wasn't going to blend into the family and have a good time? Had her brother shown up with an ulterior motive?

Thinking back to her childhood, Doris remembered how close she and Joel had once been. Back then she'd gotten along better with him than either Elsie or Arlene. Of course, she was closer to Joel's age, and they'd had a few things in common. Not anymore, though. There was nothing about Joel that reminded Doris of the closeness they'd once had. Going English had changed him, and in her opinion, not for the better.

She sighed, remembering how when they were children she'd seen Joel many times sneak up the hill to sit on the large rocks by the big oak tree. Since Joel had left, she sometimes walked up to his rock-seat when she was visiting Dad and sat awhile. It was quiet there, with a lot of activity from birds and animals. Doris felt drawn to its calming effect. She also felt closer to Joel when she sat on his rocks. Sometimes, she would close her eyes and pray that her brother would see the light and admit the error of his ways.

But it may never happen, she reminded herself. *Joel might always remain self-centered and disinterested in his family.*

Uncle Joel, did you bring your harmonica with you tonight?" The question from Arlene's twelve-year-old son, Doug, cut into Doris's thoughts.

Startled, Joel blinked a couple of times. "Uh, no. . .I didn't think to bring it." He forked a piece of chicken and plopped it on his plate.

Doug's dark eyebrows furrowed. "That's too bad. It woulda been nice to hear you and Grandpa play together again."

Elsie smiled. "You should bring it the next time you come."

Scott tugged on Joel's sleeve. "Will ya teach me how to play the harmonica, Uncle Joel?"

"Maybe sometime," Joel replied. "But you should really ask your grandpa. You see him all the time; I don't come here that often."

"And whose fault is that?" Doris spoke up. She couldn't hold her tongue any longer. "You don't really live that far from us, Joel. There's no reason you can't take the time to visit at least once a month."

All heads turned to look at Doris. She'd probably said too much, and worst of all, in front of the children. "I–I'm sorry," she murmured. "I spoke out of turn."

Arlene reached over and patted Doris's arm. "It's okay. We've all said things we wish we hadn't."

"What we need is a change of subject," Brian put in. "Eustace, why don't you tell how you singed your beard?"

Doris appreciated her husband's attempt to lighten the mood, but Dad had previously told most of them about the mishap with his beard. If he explained how it happened now, it would only be for her brother's sake. And so far, Joel didn't seem interested in much of anything being said this evening.

"Maybe Dad would rather not discuss it." Doris glanced in her father's direction. "Should we talk about something else instead?"

He shook his head. "No, that's okay. I don't mind tellin' the story again. It's good for a laugh."

While Dad recounted the details of his grilling mishap, Doris concentrated on finishing her meal.

"If it's alright with everyone, I think we'll wait awhile to have dessert," Elsie suggested when supper was over. "I ate too much and need time for my food to settle."

"That's fine by me." John thumped his stomach. "I'll enjoy my dessert a lot more if I eat it later."

All heads nodded in agreement, even the children's.

Joel glanced at his dad, wondering if he would settle into his easy chair in the living room or head outside for some fresh air. It would be a lot easier to talk to him if he went outdoors. Joel worried about what he would do if he couldn't get Dad alone tonight. He sure couldn't blurt out in front of everyone that he was in a jam and wanted to borrow some money. On the other hand, he didn't want to leave here without asking Dad.

Joel felt a surge of hope when Dad pushed away from the dining-room table and said he was going out to the barn to check on the mare that had given birth this morning.

"Mind if I tag along?" Joel asked.

Dad hesitated a moment, but finally shrugged. "Suit yourself."

Relieved that none of the other men

or any of the boys had offered to join them, Joel followed his dad out the door. When they entered the barn, he decided to make some idle conversation first, to break the ice. It would be best if he eased into the topic of money, rather than blurting it out.

They talked about Dad's horses awhile and moved on to discussing the warm weather they'd been having.

"I, for one, will be glad when summer's over and the cooler weather swoops in." Joel leaned against the mare's stall, watching her foal nurse.

Dad merely grunted in response as he chewed on a piece of straw.

"Sorry to hear you lost part of your beard, but it'll grow back, right?"

Dad nodded.

Joel stood quietly, watching him check the mare and her colt over good.

Guess it's now or never. I need to ask for the money while I have the chance.

Joel was on the verge of telling Dad his predicament when Arlene showed up. "I came out to tell you the desserts have been set on the table. Everyone's waiting for you. Seems they all have room now." She smiled at Dad. "Elsie made your favorite peach pie, so you'd better hurry before it's all gone."

Dad didn't have to be asked twice. Without so much as a word to Joel, he hurried from the barn.

"Great," Joel mumbled. At this rate he might never get to talk to Dad alone.

CHAPTER 10

"W hy don't we start a bonfire out back?" Larry suggested as they all sat around the table, eating their pie. "I'm sure the kinner would enjoy roasting some marshmallows."

"Good idea. It'll give us more time to visit with Joel," Elsie said.

Joel shook his head. "I should probably get going, but I do need to talk to Dad before I go."

"Why don't you spend the night here?" Arlene suggested. "You don't have to rush off, and it'll give you more time to spend with Dad."

Joel glanced at his father to get his reaction. If he stayed the night, he could get up before the Saturday morning traffic became heavy. With it being the final weekend in August and children soon starting a new school year, travelers would be crowding the highways for those last-minute family vacations. Joel figured if he left at sunup, he'd make it back to Akron in plenty of time to go to his bank, which was open until noon— that is, if he had a check to deposit. Everything hinged on Dad's willingness to loan him the money.

Dad looked at Joel and shrugged his shoulders. "If you wanna stay, it's fine by me."

"Really? I—I mean, I'm fine with it, too." Joel looked at Doris and noticed her scowl. Did she disapprove of him spending the night? Didn't he have the right to spend time with Dad? It didn't matter what Doris thought. Joel was an adult and could make his own decisions. Besides, if he stayed overnight, he'd have Dad all to himself and would be able to talk privately with him.

He looked at his watch, wondering whether he should give Kristi a call. In the message he had left earlier, he'd told her he would be home sometime this evening. He hoped she wouldn't call while he was here with all the family, because he'd have a hard time explaining all the background noise.

"I need to step outside and make a quick phone call," Joel stated after he finished his coffee.

"While you're making your call, I'll get the fire going." Larry jumped up and followed Joel out the door. Several others did as well.

Stepping into the night air felt nice after being inside where it was stuffy. No one else seemed to have minded the heat, so maybe only Joel felt as if he couldn't breathe. It made sense, with him being the center of attention, even among his own family, and feeling like the outsider he was.

The stars, Joel noticed, were far more intense out here at Dad's place then back home in the city where Kristi lived. Joel's own piece of land would also be a great place for star-gazing if not for all the lights he had around the place to discourage trespassing or a burglary.

Joel paused on the porch a few minutes, watching the fireflies rising from the lawn. Since July was normally the best month to see lightning bugs, he was surprised to still see a few around. Maybe it was because the nights hadn't turned cooler yet.

He breathed in the refreshing night air and for several seconds watched his family mingle. Joel waited until everyone had headed around to the back of the house where Dad's fire pit was located. Then, feeling the need for some privacy, he slipped away to make his call to Kristi.

Joel hopped into his truck and closed the door. When he took out his cell, he grimaced. The phone had no bars. "Should have known I would be off the grid way out here," he grumbled. "Guess I'd better make my way to Dad's phone shack and call Kristi from there."

Joel stepped out of his truck and was

halfway down the driveway, when his nephew, Scott called, "Where ya goin' Uncle Joel?"

Joel turned around, cupping his hands around his mouth. "I need to make a phone call. Save me a seat by the fire, okay?"

Scott bobbed his head, then darted off to join the other children playing near the barn.

When Joel entered the phone shack, a sense of nostalgia swept over him, the way it had when he'd been in the barn earlier this evening. When he and Doris were children, playing hide-and-seek, he'd sometimes hidden in the phone shack. Of course, once she'd caught on to his secret hiding place, that was the end of it.

Pulling his thoughts back to the task at hand, Joel punched in Kristi's number. She answered on the second ring.

"Hi Joel. Are you back in town?" Kristi asked cheerfully.

"No, not yet. In fact, I won't be back till sometime tomorrow morning."

"Really? But you told me you'd be back this evening."

"I know, but my business here took longer than I figured. So rather than coming home tonight, I decided it would be best to wait till morning. I'd feel better being fresh and alert when I drive home."

"That makes sense if you're too far away. Where are you anyway?" she asked.

Joel bit his lip. "Umm. . .a little south of Berlin."

"You're in Amish country?"

"Uh, yeah, that's right."

"Lucky you. Wish I had gone with you. I had so much fun the day Mom and I visited there. I'd really like to go back again."

Tap. Tap. Tap.

Joel opened the door and poked his head out. There stood Scott, looking up at him with inquisitive blue eyes. The boy opened his mouth, as if to say something, but Joel spoke first. "I'll be there soon," he whispered, then quickly shut the door.

"Who are you talking to, Joel?" Kristi questioned.

"Uh, no one. I mean, I was talking to you. Just said I'd see you soon."

Joel heard Kristi's intake of air, then waited as she paused before continuing. Kristi's voice was above a whisper when she asked, "Is everything alright, Joel? Your voice sounds strained."

"I'm fine. My job has me preoccupied, is all."

"Okay. I'll let you go. See you sometime tomorrow, Joel."

"Sounds good. I'll drop by your place tomorrow evening." Hoping to reassure her, he added, "Maybe we can go for a run before supper."

"That'd be nice, and I'd be happy to fix whatever you want to eat."

"Okay. We'll talk about it then. See you tomorrow, Kristi." Joel pressed his fingers on the receiver as he pinched his lips together. He missed Kristi and wished he were with her right now.

When Joel headed toward the bonfire, another childhood memory came to mind. Teasing Doris, he'd roasted a marshmallow for her and deliberately made sure it was well-done, to the point of turning black. He'd realized quickly she hadn't been riled one little bit, as she had let it be known how she much liked her marshmallows overly toasted. Joel could still see Doris's smug expression as she ate the ash-covered marshmallow and smacked her lips, with gooey stuff still stuck to her fingers.

I wonder how she'd respond if I made her a burned marshmallow tonight. Bet she wouldn't smile and say she liked it. Pushing his memories aside, Joel took a seat beside Scott to enjoy the rest of the evening.

Akron

Kristi settled into a wicker chair on her deck to watch the sun set in the Ohio skies. Toying with the braid she'd plated into her hair, an uneasy feeling enveloped her. Why was it she felt Joel had been keeping something from her? Or was it only her imagination running wild and making her feel uneasy?

Kristi picked up the book of crossword puzzles she'd bought a few days ago. Maybe this would keep her mind occupied. In the past, exercising her brain while working the puzzles had helped her relax. Tonight, though, she wasn't so sure.

Kristi got the first couple of words right away, but it wasn't long before her concentration faltered. She chewed on the end of her pencil and stared out across the yard. She noticed the trees had a worn-out look during their last stages of summer growth. Kristi couldn't wait for autumn. She enjoyed watching the leaves turn brilliant with color. But now, as she looked at their dull appearance, she couldn't help comparing them to her relationship with Joel. Lately it seemed their connection with each other was dull and lacked the luster they'd shared when they first started dating. Like the last autumn leaves letting go, was their relationship fading and drawing to a close? Or was it only the stress Joel felt from his job putting distance between them?

Kristi put the crossword puzzle aside. The sun had already dripped below the horizon, and the first stars were coming to light. Closing her eyes and bowing her head, she sent up a silent prayer: *Lord, please be with Joel tonight. And if our relationship is failing, and it's somehow my fault, show me how to make things better.*

Charm

The house seemed quiet after everyone went home. Eustace wondered if he should go to bed or visit with Joel awhile. He didn't have to wonder long, for Joel quickly engaged him in conversation.

"I need to ask you something, Dad." Joel took a seat on the couch.

"Oh, what about?" Eustace seated himself in his easy chair and reclined it. He was tired from the excitement of the evening and needed to relax.

Joel leaned forward, elbows on his knees. "I'm in a bit of a financial jam right now."

"What else is new? I thought you said at the dinner table that you were doing substantially well in your business." It was all Eustace could do not to point a finger at his son and exclaim what he'd been wondering all along. But he realized it would be best to keep to himself what he suspected about Joel coming home for more reasons than to visit. Eustace could almost count on the next words out of Joel's mouth, when he'd worked up his nerve to ask for something.

"I was doing well, but something messed me up, and now I'm overextended. So I was wondering if I could borrow some money."

"How much?"

"Twenty-five thousand dollars."

Eustace pulled the lever on his chair so hard it nearly propelled him out. "Are you kidding, Joel? Why do you need so much money?"

"I owe some of my subcontractors." Joel rose to his feet and moved to stand in front of Eustace. "I'll pay it back as soon as my next big job comes in."

Eustace shook his head determinedly. "Absolutely not! It upsets me that the only time you feel the need to come around is when you want something."

Joel's cheeks reddened as he ran a shaky

hand through his hair. "It may seem that way, but—"

"Do I need to remind you that the last time you came here you borrowed money but never paid it back? Now you have the nerve to ask my help again." Eustace lifted both hands. "You're profligate."

"Huh?"

"You're reckless. When are you gonna grow up and take responsibility for yourself?"

Joel's eyes narrowed. "I'll bet if it was one of my sisters asking for money you'd give it to her with no hesitation."

"I may, but none of your sisters are as irresponsible as you. For the most part, they're magnanimous."

"Magnanimous? What's that supposed to mean?"

"Worthy and upright. If they owed me money, you can be sure they'd pay it back."

"I'll pay my debt to you—for the last loan, as well as this one. Please give me another chance." Joel's tone was pleading.

Eustace held his ground. If he gave in, his son would never learn to stand on his own two feet. "You're spoiled, and it's time you grew up and took responsibility for your mistakes without expecting me to come to your rescue. It's not like you care about your family anyway." His tone was flat.

"I do care. I made a mistake and need some money to tide me over till another big job comes along."

"I suspected during supper, actually, that you were up to something." Eustace crossed his arms. "You can't fool me, Joel. A father knows his child's heart. You have truly strayed and need to change the path you're on before you lose any more of your precious money. A man like you will never be affluent, because he loses what he has as soon as he acquires it."

"But—but Dad. . ."

Eustace held up his hand. "Sorry, Son, but you won't be leaving here with a check from me. I will give you no more money. And don't come back here again unless it's strictly to visit. You're not being fair to the rest of the family."

"Fine then! If that's the way you feel, I won't come back at all!" Joel stomped toward the door then turned back around with his index finger in the air. "By the way, those big words you've been using don't make you any smarter than me!" He went to the door again and swung it open, letting it slam behind him.

Eustace sank back into his chair. It hadn't been easy telling Joel no, seeing such a look of desperation on his face. Like most parents, it was in Eustace's nature to want to help his children and see them succeed. But Joel would never learn the value of a dollar or the importance of family if he had everything handed to him. What Joel needed was to follow the example of his brothers-in-law and quit blowing money on things he didn't need. Eustace felt sure that's exactly what had happened. No doubt his son had bought something he couldn't afford, and probably with someone else's money. *Will my son ever stop being so selfish? How far down will he travel before he hits rock bottom? What Joel needs to do is a sincere, selfless act.*

Joel ground his teeth as he headed straight for his truck, never bothering to look back. Struggling with his emotions, he drove out and stopped up at the top of the hill, where he parked and turned off the engine. His dad's harsh voice still rang in his ears, drowning out the relentless chorus of the katydid's rhythmic song, as he stared out the front window into the blackness of night.

He pounded the steering wheel until his hands ached. As Joel calmed down, he rested his arms and head on the wheel and berated himself. *What did I think would happen tonight? I knew Dad would react like he did, but I had to try.* He felt alone and defeated. Without help from Dad, how was he going to pay his subcontractors?

Joel peered down at the now-dark farmhouse. No doubt Dad was sleeping soundly, unconcerned about how he'd refused to help. "He's probably snoring in 'la-la' land and not thinking anymore about me right now." He pounded the steering wheel again, this time accidently honking the horn. "So what if I woke Dad up?" He winced. "I'm his only son. How can he do this to me?"

Joel agonized over his dilemma for a while, but realizing he needed to get home, he started up his truck. *I do care about my family*, he told himself. *They—especially Dad—don't really care about me.*

As Joel headed down the road toward home, his thoughts ran wild, increasing his anger. *Who does Dad think he is, treating me like that? If I had a son who came to me with a need, I'd give him whatever he wanted, no questions asked.*

Joel turned on the radio, trying to drown out his thoughts, but it was no use. He could still hear Dad accusing him of being selfish.

As Joel approached the entrance to the freeway outside of Dover, a car coming from the opposite direction swerved into his lane. Before Joel could react, the vehicle slammed into his truck. The last thing Joel felt was searing pain. Then his world faded into blackness.

Wanda E. Brunstetter

New York Times bestselling author, Wanda E. Brunstetter is one of the founders of the Amish fiction genre. Wanda's ancestors were part of the Anabaptist faith, and her novels are based on personal research intended to accurately portray the Amish way of life. Her books are well-read and trusted by many Amish, who credit her for giving readers a deeper understanding of the people and their customs. When Wanda visits her Amish friends, she finds herself drawn to their peaceful life-style, sincerity, and close family ties. Wanda enjoys photography, ventriloquism, garden-ing, bird-watching, beachcombing, and spending time with her family. She and her husband, Richard, have been blessed with two grown children, six grandchildren, and two great-grandchildren.

To learn more about Wanda, visit her website at www.wandabrunstetter.com.

Jean Brunstetter

Jean Brunstetter became fascinated with the Amish when she first went to Pennsylvania to visit her father-in-law's family. Since that time, Jean has become friends with several Amish families and enjoys writing about their way of life. She also likes to put some of the simple practices followed by the Amish into her daily routine. Jean lives in Washington State with her husband, Richard Jr. and their three children, but takes every opportunity to visit Amish communities in several states. In addition to writing, Jean enjoys boating, gardening, and spending time on the beach.

The Story Of The Amish Millionaire Continues With…

The Stubborn Father, part two of *The Amish Millionaire* saga, widower Eustace Byler stands out in his Amish community for his eccentricity and his wealth. He mourns the loss of his son to the world like he mourns the physical loss of his wife. In the past, Eustace has freely loaned Joel money, perhaps hoping to entice him back home, but now Eustace is done and moving on to fulfill some of his own dreams.

Don't Miss a Single Book In This Exclusive 6-Book Serial Novel

AVAILABLE AT YOUR FAVORITE BOOKSTORE